Their Unexpected Love
Kathleen Y'Barbo

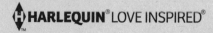

Recycling programs
for this product may
not exist in your area.

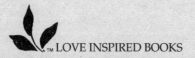 LOVE INSPIRED BOOKS

ISBN-13: 978-0-373-87900-7

THEIR UNEXPECTED LOVE

www.Harlequin.com

Printed in U.S.A.

"I work with kids that aren't always considered socially acceptable," Pippa said.

She glanced at Logan and continued, "I'm wondering whether you thought those kids were up to no good based on how they looked."

"Partly," he said. "If I remember right, the rest of what I said was that they reminded me of myself at that age. I wasn't exactly socially acceptable, either."

Pippa nodded. "That's why I'm so passionate about the skating outreach. These kids are outcasts, or at least they look like it, and they need a place to go where they're off the streets."

"I don't think that would have worked for me, so I'm not sure I can agree with your method."

She opened her mouth to argue and then decided taking a bite of pie was the better course of action. Obviously Logan's opinions and hers were in direct opposition.

He met her gaze. Oh, but the man was handsome, even if he was completely wrong about the best way to win wayward souls to the Lord.

Books by Kathleen Y'Barbo

Love Inspired

*Daddy's Little Matchmakers
*Her Holiday Fireman
*Their Unexpected Love

*Second Time Around

KATHLEEN Y'BARBO

is a multipublished bestselling author of Christian fiction and nonfiction with over thirty books to her credit. She writes historical novels for Waterbrook Press and is the coauthor of two nonfiction books on divorce and empty-nest syndrome. A tenth-generation Texan, she holds a marketing degree from Texas A&M University and a certificate in paralegal studies. Kathleen is the proud mother of a daughter and three grown sons.

How, then, can they call on the one they have not believed in? And how can they believe in the one of whom they have not heard? And how can they hear without someone preaching to them?
—*Romans* 10:14

For skaters and their parents.
And to my skaters,
Andrew and Jacob Y'Barbo....
And finally, thank you to the real Logan
for allowing me to borrow your name.

Chapter One

Every detail of this afternoon's fund-raiser for the Vine Beach Senior Center had been handled well beforehand, leaving Pippa Gallagher with plenty of time to scan the crowd. It appeared that everyone who was anyone in this little slice of Texas beach had accepted the invitation to come and bid on originals and prints of the celebrated artist Pearl.

Because the last children's book Granny had worked on was set on Oahu, Pippa had settled on a party to match. The tropical theme had gone over well, as evidenced by the plethora of citizens dressed in floral attire that made the room look as if it were a neon garden. The addition of palm trees and tropical touches to Granny's otherwise traditional décor gave the oversize reception room an island feel. With the doors thrown open, the sea air and sounds of the waves crashing nearby added to the ambience.

Waitstaff in Hawaiian garb passed through the crowd, offering fruit drinks and appetizers while Don Ho's ukulele music played softly through the sound system. Though Pippa had borrowed the ideas from an oil company executive's retirement party she had planned before she'd left the corporate world, the addition of Granny's paintings and the mayor in the costume of a Hawaiian chief was all Vine Beach. Mayor Murdoch caught her watching and lifted his spear in greeting.

"How you managed to get that man to wear that outfit is beyond me, Pippa."

She turned to see her friend Leah Berry-Owen grinning. "The same way I got Pop's Seafood Shack to provide the sushi."

Leah chuckled. "Pop would have a fit if he knew any fish was leaving his kitchen in a condition other than fried or grilled."

"It's just for the party," Pippa reminded the restaurant's owner. "Unless you're considering putting it on the menu. The guests are certainly enjoying it."

"It does seem to be disappearing." Leah's gaze slid past her to fix on something near the door. "And speaking of disappearing, look who is back in Vine Beach. And at a party, no less."

"What do you mean?" Pippa turned in the direction that her companion indicated but found her view blocked. "Who's back?"

"Well, I mean Ryan said he'd been going to Starting Over group for the last couple of months, so technically I knew he was back, but this is the first time I've seen him out socially." Leah paused to address Pippa. "You know about Starting Over, right?"

Pippa nodded. She had indeed heard of the church-sponsored widowers' group and of Leah's husband's history, first as a member and now as a mentor.

"His father probably made him go, what with his practically founding the group. Still…" She craned her neck to look at the subject of her musings and then returned her attention to Pippa. "I'm just surprised he's here, that's all.

I mean, even though it's been almost two years since…
Oh, he's coming this way."

"He? Leah, who are you talking about?" Pippa turned
around but a broad shoulder kept her from seeing anything. By tipping her head up, she looked directly into
the pale green eyes of Logan Burkett. "Oh."

Swallowing hard, she took in high, tanned cheekbones
and thick black lashes ringing eyes the color of beach
glass. Caramel-colored hair streaked in places by the sun
curled at the edge of the collar of his white button-down
shirt. Faded jeans and boots gave the impression of a
cowboy who had found a luau while looking for a rodeo.

His eyes darted past her as he smiled. "Leah Berry,
right?" Logan extended his hand, and Leah shook it.

"Owen, actually. Or rather Berry-Owen. I married
Ryan almost a year ago now." Leah's attention flitted to
Pippa, her expression exhorting her to say something.
Anything.

Seeing Logan Burkett again after all these years
shouldn't have given Pippa a swarm of butterflies in her
stomach. What was it about the man that made her feel
as if she were still that goofy ninth grader with the awkward hairstyle and the complete inability to fit in?

Maybe it was the fact that Logan had changed very little since she'd last seen him. Oh, he was older, definitely
sporting muscles that weren't there back in high school.
But he was still the good-looking guy with the attitude
that told the world he knew it and the oh-so-handsome
face that backed it up.

He grinned, and her stomach did a flip. *Oh.*

Making a face at Pippa's prolonged silence, Leah continued. "Logan, you remember Pippa Gallagher from
Vine Beach High, don't you?" Now she smiled directly
at her friend. "Pippa, this is Logan Burkett."

Pippa reached to shake his hand and found his grip firm, his hands showing the calluses of a working man. "Welcome back to Vine Beach," she said, an absurd statement considering she herself had just returned a few months ago.

"Well, thank you," he said, "but we've already met."

"No," Pippa said quickly. "I would have remembered." The words, once out, made her cringe.

"B and B Construction?" He shook his head. "Surely you remember the guy you've been emailing with for the past month."

"LB?"

As in Logan Burkett. From ninth grade. The guy whose head probably still bore the scars of her skateboard falling out of the locker above his. The one with whom she had debated everything from ambient lighting and reclaimed floor tiles to low-flush toilets?

"Yes, that's me. Guess I should have spelled out my whole name, but I don't have much patience for emails." A shrug. "Besides, with Vine Beach being such a small town, I figured you knew."

"Wait a minute," Leah said. "You're her…"

"Construction foreman on the remodel? Yes, that's me. I've sent her a construction update email every Friday at noon for the past four weeks."

"Punctual," Leah whispered when Logan looked away. "I like that in a man. And, girl, he is cute, too."

Pippa nudged her friend and then gave her a look that, of course, Leah ignored. "Behave," she added as a useless afterthought.

Leah would never behave. Not when it meant giving up a chance to find a man for Pippa. Just because Leah was happily married to the handsome fire marshal, she did not have a license to send Pippa toward the altar.

The music on the sound system switched to a Beach Boys tune, a distraction that lasted only a second. Pippa's eyes narrowed as she thought back over the series of emails regarding the renovation of the building in downtown Vine Beach.

In a previous conversation, Granny had mentioned something about the foreman being a changed man. About finding his faith and going off to build churches in Africa and then losing it over some life tragedy, though the details on both were a bit vague. Perhaps she should have paid more attention.

Had Pippa known Granny was rattling on about Logan Burkett, she certainly would have.

"Pippa?" Leah nudged her. "You're staring," she whispered. "Stop it." And then she turned to Logan. "So, tell me what you're doing for my silent friend here. Rumor around town is the old bakery is going to be Mrs. Gallagher's showplace. I can't even get Pippa to tell me what the plans are."

"There's nothing to tell because the plans haven't been finalized yet," Pippa said as she found her voice.

"About that," Logan said. "I had an idea on the way over that I'd like to talk to you about when you get a chance."

"Before our meeting with Granny?"

A shrug. "Doesn't have to be."

"All right. I'll check my schedule and email you." Again she fought the blush that should have gone with such a ridiculous statement. Until Granny's art gallery opened on the first floor of the building Logan was remodeling, Pippa's schedule was light at best. Except for planning this event, the only actual work she'd done was over at the skate park.

Not that she considered building a ministry where kids

could come and in-line skate or skateboard in a safe environment work. That was pure fun.

"It looks like the church will get its senior center after all," Logan said.

Leah grinned. "With Pippa in charge, there was never a doubt. Did you know she was quite successful in her former career as a corporate events planner and fundraiser?"

Pippa felt the heat flood her cheeks. What was wrong with her? This was her building contractor, not a potential prom date.

"Really, Leah," Pippa said. "I doubt Logan is interested in all that."

"I can see my friend doesn't want to brag," Leah said. "And as much as I would love to fill you in on all the details of her illustrious career, as owner of the company chosen to offer sushi to the masses this afternoon, I should circulate and do a little quality control." She eyed Logan before resting her attention on Pippa. "I'll call you later."

Before Pippa could comment, Leah was gone, blending into the crowd. Slowly Pippa met Logan's impassive gaze. Goodness but his eyes were a beautiful shade of green.

"You planned all this?" He nodded toward the crowd. "Impressive."

"It's what I do." Pippa reached out to snatch a festive-looking glass of pineapple-orange punch from a passing waiter. "Or rather what I did before Granny decided she needed me closer to home."

"So you're taking care of your grandmother now?"

"Taking care of Granny? No," she said with a chuckle. "Hardly. If anything it's the other way around. I think she was lonely and wanted me home." Her gaze traveled around the room, then settled back on Logan. "She has plenty of friends but I'm all the family she's got here in Vine Beach."

"Well, it's nice that you're back anyway. It takes someone special to put a career on hold for a family member." Logan gave her a direct look. "About high school. I have to ask. Was I awful to you?"

His question caught her off guard. It was almost as if he had changed the subject deliberately. Being ignored in high school wasn't awful if the recipient wished she were invisible. And Logan's claiming back then to hate skateboards was fair since he had been hit enough times as they fell from the locker above.

So she said, "No," as she twirled the drink's pink paper umbrella with her index finger.

"Good." Relief punctuated the statement. "On the way here I saw kids dressed like they were up to no good. Reminded me of myself at that age. Not a good feeling to know I was one of them."

One of *them?*

Pippa bristled at the statement she'd heard far too often in relation to the kids at the skate park, kids who loved Jesus but looked different. As she once did.

"What do you mean exactly?" she asked carefully.

"I've spent a whole lot of years apologizing for the jerk I was back then."

Not the answer to her question. "I would hate to be judged by what I did in ninth grade. Or what I looked like." The latter was a carefully aimed dig at his assumption that kids' clothing somehow reflected their hearts.

"You look like sunshine right now," he said, then glanced away. "Sorry, that sounded really stupid. Anyway," he added abruptly, "I appreciate the invitation today. I don't usually go to these things, but your grandmother can be persuasive."

The oddest sensation came over Pippa as she watched Logan Burkett's obvious discomfort. Apparently anyone could feel out of place given the right set of circumstances. Even the most popular boy at Vine Beach High School.

The silence between them lengthened until Pippa felt compelled to fill it. "I don't know too many people in Vine Beach anymore. Just a few old friends are still here. Most have moved on."

"Seems that way."

Another conversational dead end. Pippa's eyes swept the crowd and then stalled on the town veterinarian and his wife, both good friends since her teen years. Eric made no pretense of not watching the two of them, although he seemed more concerned with Logan and what he might be doing here. Just as it appeared the veterinarian was headed her way, Granny waylaid him and they began conversing.

Pippa took a sip to fortify her dry mouth only to somehow manage to jab the end of the pink paper umbrella up her nose. With the back of her hand, Pippa swatted it away and saw it spiral out of sight to land beside a spray of orchids and a stack of Granny's books.

Thankfully Logan seemed too preoccupied with the crowd milling around them to notice. Still, heat flamed her cheeks as she took a healthy gulp of juice.

By the time she managed a somewhat neutral expression, Logan was grinning. So he had seen her embarrass herself. If only the ground would just swallow her up.

"This is a beautiful home," Logan offered. "Guessing it'll be hard to move out when the building is finished."

"Actually I don't live here," she said. "Granny would

like me to, but that feels a little too much like high school, so I'm renting Leah Owen's beachfront place until the loft is ready."

"Which won't take long," he said quickly.

"Oh, I'm not complaining," Pippa said. "I love living right on the beach. There's just something about seeing the waves crashing and…" She shook her head as she waved away the statement. "Anyway, it will be nice to live just around the corner from where I work, so I'll also be happy when I'm settled downtown."

"Around the corner?" Logan gave her a look. "Won't you be living upstairs from where you work?"

"Oh, yes," she quickly corrected. "Once the gallery is open. And it will be nice to live there," Pippa added. "Great architecture will trump sandy feet, I suppose."

"The sand's not that far away. Just a couple of blocks." Logan paused. "So where are you working now?"

"R10:14 Skate Park," she said. "Though I don't actually *work* there. I'm a volunteer."

"Skate park?" He chuckled. "That's funny."

Pippa stood a little straighter. "What's so funny about it?"

His smile faded. "Well, you don't exactly look like the skateboarding type."

"Now I know you don't remember me from high school. Maybe it was all those times my skateboard fell out of my locker and hit you on your head. I always wondered if you left Vine Beach High the next year because of that."

He gave her a sideways look. Slowly recognition dawned as his gaze swept the length of her. "But you're too…"

Oh, this was fun. "I'm too what?" At his stricken expression, Pippa elected to give the poor guy a break. "If you were about to say that I am too pretty to be a skateboarder, then I would have to say thank you. If, however, you were about to say something else, then I retract the thanks."

"You've got me there. And you're welcome."

Logan waved a waiter over and picked up a glass of juice. Before he handed it to Pippa, he removed the yellow umbrella and stuck it in his front pocket.

Their eyes met, Logan looking amused. And then, just barely, one corner of his mouth lifted in the beginning of a grin.

"So, about the building," Pippa said. "Granny has a meeting with you to finalize the details on her calendar, right?"

"She does, though if you want I can send the details to you via email."

"No need," she said. "Our calendars are synched so the appointment reminder will be there when I get to work on Monday. I'm curious, though. Have you found any surprises during the demolition?"

"So far, no. The old building is solid as a rock. It just needs a little work, at least upstairs where you'll be living. Downstairs is going to take more time, but that's something we've already discussed." Logan's expression was tentative. "You said you like your view of the ocean in the rental. That reminds me of the idea I had."

Granny stepped into view, Vine Beach's mayor at her side. Apparently the part of the evening Pippa most dreaded was about to get under way. How many times had she smiled until her jaws ached at these events? Too many to count.

The irony was that while she loved to plan events, she had short tolerance for actually attending them.

"I'm curious," she said to Logan. "What's your idea? Some kind of decorating thing?"

He gave her a wide-eyed look. "Do I look like a deco-rator?" When she laughed, he continued. "It's a construc-tion item." Uncertainty showed in his expression. "I spied some minor damage from last night's storm that's going to have to be repaired. While I was digging around—"

"Ladies and gentlemen" came the booming voice of Mayor Murdoch. "Can I have your attention? We came here for a reason, and I think it's time we got started."

Logan shrugged as if to indicate his inability to con-tinue. Pippa gave her attention to the mayor, who was accepting a hug from Granny before handing her the microphone.

"Every one of you is here because you've indicated an interest in what the Gallagher Trust is doing," Granny said. "For this I want to thank you. When my late hus-band and I set up this trust, I never expected the Lord would use it so mightily to bless others."

Pippa thought of all the good her grandparents had done over the years and smiled. Not only had they funded her parents in their mission work in Indonesia, but they also sent out scores of others who had gone out to do the work of the Lord. And without the small stipend the trust paid her, she'd never have been able to get the youth min-istry she called R10:14 up and running.

"So, Mayor," Granny continued, "why don't you do the honors and tell us who will be going home with my paintings tonight?"

Pippa stifled a groan. *Here we go.* If she didn't find a way out soon, she would eventually be drawn into the speech-giving. Or, the way she thought of it, the mo-ment when everyone stared and she made a fool of her-self by either babbling nonsensically or finding nothing to say at all.

The mayor took the microphone and began to wax

poetic on the tight competition for coveted pieces of art from the Gallagher collection. Every painting had a name and a story attached, and the politician took great care to draw out each before declaring the winners.

Pippa caught Logan watching her, then grinned when he quickly looked away. Apparently he shared her desire to escape.

Across the room, Dr. Wilson's name was announced as the winner of Granny's *Sailboats at Dawn* painting. By Pippa's count there were at least two dozen more pieces to award. And then would come the speeches.

Time to make a discreet exit.

"So," she whispered when she caught Logan's attention again. "I was just leaving. Want to join me? You could show me that construction add-on you were talking about."

"Now?" Recognition dawned as Logan leaned close. "You're not exactly dressed for walking around a construction site."

"Neither are you." She gestured to the surfboard-themed tie he wore. "I don't mind if you don't."

A glance around the room and Logan returned his attention to her with a grin. "Are you kidding? Let's go."

Chapter Two

Pippa led the way around the back of Granny's house, skirting the pool and the outdoor kitchen to enter the service area that led to the garage. Kicking off her heels, she slipped into the sandals she kept there. While she used them for wearing out on the sandy beach or in the outdoor shower, they should also work for poking around an old building. At the very least they should keep her from falling on her face, a distinct possibility in the uncomfortable but pretty yellow shoes she'd donned for the party.

She turned to be sure Logan was still following. He'd already removed his jacket and slung it over his arm and was in the process of loosening his surfboard tie. When their gazes met, he gave her a dazzling smile.

"Kind of like skipping class," Pippa said, though she'd never dared make that sort of attempt back in high school.

"Kind of," he replied as he reached up to run a hand through his sand-colored hair. His left hand.

Instantly Pippa checked for a ring and found none, then stifled a cringe. *What is wrong with me?*

"You never skipped class, did you?" he asked.

"Never," she admitted.

"Then I suppose it's time. Lead on," said the object

of her thoughts as he loosened the top two buttons on his dress shirt.

"This way." Pippa glanced around and spied her Mini Cooper wedged between Granny's sedan and several other cars. Apparently the valets for tonight's event weren't concerned with whether the family might need to escape.

She stopped short and looked around. "The blue one's mine, but it's not going anywhere. Do you mind driving?"

"Long as you don't mind the wind in your hair," Logan said. "I didn't expect company, so I left the top to the Jeep back home in my garage."

"I'll manage."

A moment later Logan waved away a valet to gesture toward a black Jeep Wrangler parked up the road between two vehicles of a more expensive type. As promised, the top was off, exposing the seats to the elements.

"Your chariot awaits," he said as he trotted around to help her climb into the passenger seat.

Thankful she'd worn her hair up today, Pippa slid the seat belt into position and sat back to enjoy the ride. Only as the gates of Granny's neighborhood were closing behind them did she truly consider the fact that she'd just left a party with a man she hardly knew.

In Vine Beach.

In broad daylight—or rather what remained of it as the sun teased the edge of the watery horizon.

Then again, it was Vine Beach. And it was Logan Burkett, a man she'd be working closely with at least until the end of the restoration project.

Pippa let out a long breath, grasping the edges of the seat as Logan made an abrupt turn and headed up the highway toward the downtown area. A strand of hair dislodged, and she quickly tucked it back into place.

Landmarks whizzed by. First came the historic Berry-hill Farm, the Civil War–era mansion that Leah and Ryan owned. The main house on the property had been reduced to rubble after a devastating fire several years ago, so the couple now lived in a renovated caretaker's house and raised palomino horses on the lush grassland location.

Just past that on the beach side of the road was Pop's Seafood Shack and the collection of pastel-colored rental homes where she currently resided. Pippa thought to point out hers, then caught herself. No sense in giving Logan more information about her than he already knew.

So she held her comments until the cottage where Eric and Amy Wilson lived appeared in view. What was once a tiny home had been recently remodeled to include an addition that purportedly doubled the size of the home.

"Such a pretty house," she said as she watched the rose-covered trellis that marked the front walkway slip past.

"Thanks," Logan said as he spared her a glance. At her questioning look, he continued. "Amy didn't want to move, but with the new baby there wasn't enough room for the two of them and four kids."

"Yes, I know," Pippa said, having been part of the group of ladies who had given Amy her baby shower. "I didn't realize you were an architect, as well."

"I'm not." His attention remained focused on the road even as a muscle tightened in his jaw. "I just like to play around with that kind of stuff. You could say I'm self-taught."

"I see." Pippa tried to make light of what had suddenly become a touchy topic. "Well, you're very good at it. Have you ever considered going back to school and—"

"Thanks, but no, I don't think so." Logan pulled the Jeep to a stop to await the green light before turning onto

Main Street. "Look, I appreciate the compliment, but I'm doing just fine hammering nails and sawing boards."

Though his look was likely supposed to convince her otherwise, his expression told Pippa there was more to it. Had she known him any better, she might have asked. Instead she kept her silence and her curiosity.

They circled past the courthouse and then a line of buildings that stretched the distance between the Vine Beach Community Center to the north and Grace Church to the south. In between was a collection of hundred-year-old brick structures punctuated with the occasional up-start 60's-era glass front office. Smack in the middle of the entire grouping was the former Branson's Bakery, the place where Pippa would finally put down roots.

It was a good thing, she reminded herself as the familiar dread threatened. Women her age were having babies and lamenting the careers they'd given up. Thus it was high time she let go of her dream of a full-time skate park ministry and do something productive.

She would still be involved in the ministry even though her main responsibility would be to Granny and the ground-floor gallery Pippa would be managing for her. The budget allowed for the hiring of at least two part-time employees, so her evenings and weekends would still be mostly available. Pippa let out a long breath. Breaking the news to the kids who had christened her with the nickname of Flip, thanks to her skating prowess, that the R10:14's hours would be shortened was not something she'd been looking forward to.

Eventually she'd have to tell them, though. A thought occurred. Until the store was completed, her time was her own. Which meant she could spend as much of that time at the skate park as she wished.

Pippa glanced at Logan as an idea formed. "So," she

said slowly, "how long did you say the work was going to take?"

"I didn't." He signaled to turn. "But I'm thinking if I get the materials in when they've been promised, I can turn over the keys to your loft in three weeks. Two and a half if I hurry."

Unexpected disappointment hit her hard. She'd hoped for at least another month of uninterrupted time at the skate park before she had to divide herself between ministry and commerce. Two or three would be better, as it would give her time to see the teenagers had a safe place to spend their time through the summer months.

"I see," Pippa said as brightly as she could manage.

"The store itself will take a little longer. We're retrofitting what's there, so there are fewer issues with what's behind the walls. Still, I'm going to say that's another month or two of work, depending."

Her hopes rose. Several months would be wonderful. Longer, even better. "Depending?"

Logan nodded. "Never know what'll happen on a job site. Lots of variables. Until this morning I had no idea we'd be hiding a broken satellite dish." At her confused look, he continued. "Apparently the storm knocked it over. The historical commission will never approve of it dangling in full view of people on the street. Nor would your grandmother."

"True." Pippa twisted the sliver bracelet on her wrist and tried to sound casual. "And this new idea you have? Will that add to the time line?"

"At least two weeks, maybe three or four depending on what I find when my helper and I start tearing things apart. Of course, if you're in a hurry I might be able to come up with a less labor-intensive plan to speed things up."

"No," she said quickly. Too quickly, Pippa decided when her companion gave her a surprised look. "What I mean is, I'm comfortable in my rental, so there's no need to hurry," she amended. "And I know Granny will want the job done right."

"Okay, but understand I always make sure the job's done right."

Their gazes collided, and Pippa gripped the edge of the seat. Oh my, he was handsome. "Of course," she managed.

And he would. Any guy who practically had his construction updates automated to deliver at precisely noon every Friday did not seem like the type who would take shortcuts.

Logan shut off the engine and pocketed the keys. "Before we go in, there are a couple of things you need to know. First, be careful where you walk. The building's solid as a rock, but that doesn't mean the floor doesn't have some soft spots. I don't want you ending up on the first floor by any way but the stairs, got it?"

Pippa nodded as she exited the Jeep. "Got it."

"And you're not exactly wearing safety shoes, so watch out for nails. Some of the demo has already been done, so just—"

"Be careful," she said along with him. "I will. And for the record, I've done a little construction work in my time, so I'm pretty good at avoiding on-the-job injuries."

By the sound of his chuckle, Logan apparently did not realize she was serious. Maybe someday she would take him down to the R10:14 to show him how she and a few others turned the empty warehouse into a haven for skateboarders and in-line skaters. She'd certainly pounded her share of nails and gained almost as many bruises and splinters in the completion of what the kids liked to call phase one of the park.

"And for the record, I do own a pair of safety shoes," she said just as Logan closed the door.

Granny had insisted once she spied the warehouse and the work that Pippa would be doing. As a compromise, however, Pippa had allowed one of the kids to customize the ugly black boots. An expert at tagging whose efforts were now confined to the interior of R10:14 thanks to a brush with the law, one of the skaters—a fellow named Rico—had worked his magic with spray paint to give her a stunning pair of boots with her nickname emblazoned on them. She still wore them sometimes, though the need had long since passed.

Logan met her on the curb, then led the way. The redbrick facade had been scrubbed clean, and the marble cornerstone that proclaimed the name of Branson's Bakery and its opening year of 1905 now gleamed bright white.

She ran her fingertips over the carved brass plate beneath the door's arched handle, its golden color faded and in dire need of polish. "Can you imagine how many hands have touched this over the years?"

He gave her an appreciative smile as he brushed past her to unlock the door. "Come on," Logan said, and gestured toward the murky shadows of the area that had once been the bakery's showroom.

Though Pippa had walked through the building with Granny on several occasions, she'd not been inside since the renovation work began last week. After the crew had removed the awful acoustic tiles that were added some fifty years ago, the ceiling was twice the height of the rooms upstairs, giving the space an expansive feel.

"Kept the heat up near the roof," Logan said as he

brushed past her. "The tall ceilings down here, that is." He walked over to the staircase and looked up. "Too bad the apartment upstairs doesn't have these ceilings. Guess Mr. Branson didn't much care if Mrs. Branson stayed cool in the summer."

"It was likely that Mrs. Branson was down here working alongside her husband," Pippa remarked.

"You could be right," Logan said with a nod as he turned his attention toward the stairs.

While Logan studied the sturdiness of the staircase, Pippa turned around to see stripes of sunlight slanting through the dust-streaked window and racing across the worn wooden floors. Closing her eyes, she could imagine what it would have looked like new in 1905. And what it might look like again in a few months.

She opened her eyes to spy Logan looking at her. He'd draped his arm over the banister, his palm resting on the ornate newel post. "If I'd realized I'd be showing this to you today, I would have brought the preliminary drawings. After you see my idea, I'll make any updates you think would be acceptable and email the documents."

"That would be perfect," she said. "But for now, just tell me what you're thinking for this space."

Logan stepped into a shaft of sunlight and smiled. "All right, I guess we can see well enough. Over there," he said, gesturing to the far corner of the room, "is where I thought we would put the cashier's counter."

Pippa followed the direction of his gaze and nodded. As Logan continued his explanation, her attention drifted from the room in which they stood to the man who would transform it. From his sun-streaked hair to the tanned and muscled forearms showing beneath the rolled-up sleeve of his dress shirt, time had been kind to the kid who'd disappeared from Vine Beach High a year after Pippa arrived. Just about the same time her confidence in ever fitting in fled, as well.

"Pippa, are you coming?"

"Oh, sorry," she said as she hurried to follow Logan toward the once-grand staircase that snaked up the brick wall with sagging risers and more than a few missing spindles.

"I checked and it's sturdy, but step carefully," he reminded her.

Emerging onto the second-floor landing, Pippa could see demolition work had begun here, as well. Though the hardwood floor, in need of a new coat of varnish, had only been covered with paper, most of the walls were now stripped to the studs.

The difference in the amount of light and the feeling of openness was remarkable, especially in the spot she had designated as her reading corner. With a view of the beach at the far end of Main Street, the corner would have a window seat fitted neatly into a bookshelf. It was something she had dreamed of since reading *A Little Princess* and imagining what it might be like living in an attic room with dormer windows. While these were not dormers, they would do.

"Like it?" Logan asked, a pleased expression on his face.

"I love it," she said. "You were right about knocking down these walls."

"I hope you'll think that about what I brought you here to see." He nodded toward a door at the opposite end of the hall. "Come with me."

"To the attic? What's up there?" she asked, though she trailed behind him.

Logan paused halfway up the stairs to glance over his shoulder. "Just wait and see."

At the top of the stairs, he reached for a flashlight left hanging on the rafter. "Stay close behind me," he warned, "and don't walk anywhere but on these beams." He gestured to the large expanses of lumber that crisscrossed the open flooring. "Ready?"

At her nod, Logan set off. She followed a step behind. Up here the air was thick with the scent of neglect, punctuated with a musty smell that made Pippa sneeze.

He reached back to steady her. "Can't have you falling through the ceiling and landing on a perfectly good floor. Might crack the boards."

His brow rose as he waited for her giggle. Instead she sneezed again, then offered a smile. "I'm fine. Keep going," she said as she fell back into step behind him.

Logan led her to the window on the easternmost side of the attic. "This is the part that's going to take some imagination." He lifted the window sash and instantly fresh salty sea air replaced the century-old smells. "I should have asked before I brought you up here." He met her gaze. "Are you afraid of heights?"

"You've never seen me on the half-pipe," she said as she thought of the last time she'd skateboarded on the giant structure in the back of the warehouse.

Apparently Logan hadn't heard of a half-pipe. Or maybe he just couldn't imagine her on one. Either way, his expression remained blank.

"The answer would be no, I'm not," she added.

A nod, and Logan reached outside the window to lean to the right. "This is the fire escape. The ladder's completely safe. Even the fire marshal agrees."

Logan's mention of Ryan Owen, Vine Beach's fire marshal, reminded Pippa that she needed to stop by and pick up the check for the specially designed Bibles he and Leah were donating to next Saturday's skating event at R10:14.

"Pippa?" He looked down at her feet. "You're probably going to need to kick off those sandals for this. Construction debris won't be a problem where we're going."

Putting aside thoughts of tomorrow, she shrugged. "And where is that, dare I ask?"

His grin was immediate. "The roof."

Pippa did as he asked, then watched as he slipped out the window and onto the fire escape. The breeze that she'd smelled inside now whipped against her as she gripped the warm metal handles of the ladder.

At the top of the stairs, Logan offered her his hand and she took it. "Turn around."

She did and then gasped. From where she stood, she could see all of Vine Beach. From the lighthouse and marina to the high school and the farmland beyond, the expansive vista was astonishing.

"Oh, Logan. It's beautiful." Her eyes caught the sharp drop-off at the edge of the building and her stomach did a flip-flop. "Kind of dangerous, though, don't you think?"

"As it is now, I wouldn't recommend spending time up here," he said. "If I were to put up a rail over there and bring up a staircase through an entrance in the roof over there with planters circling the perimeter, I could make this a nice rooftop deck. Minus the satellite dish, which really ought to be taken down." He paused and seemed to be waiting for her opinion.

Pippa took it all in, the ideas, the view and the enthusiasm of the man beside her. "Yes," she agreed as her gaze fixed on a familiar sight—the roof of the warehouse that housed R10:14. "I like it, but I wonder if just a deck is enough." She tore her attention away from the warehouse and fixed it on Logan. "What about some sort of arbor?

Or trellis? Something to shade part of the roof from the sun. If we're going to do this I'd really like it to look more like an oasis than just a plain deck."

Logan's grin was slow but worth the wait. "Definitely," he said. "I can draw something up, but every project you add will take extra time."

She gave the area another sweeping glance. "Take all the time you need, Logan," she said. "I'm in no hurry at all."

"Are you sure your grandmother will go for this extra expense? Not only are we talking about more time and materials, but there are also the costs for getting the blueprints altered. Then there will be another trip before the city council to get everything approved." He shrugged. "The only good part is that so far the building has not been claimed by the historical commission. If that were to happen before we turned in the plans, everything would take much longer."

Pippa contemplated asking how to get the building put under consideration by the commission and then decided it might be too obvious. "Leave Granny to me," she said instead. "Just get busy planning something amazing."

"Amazing," Logan echoed. "Got it. And you're sure you don't mind the extra time this thing will take?"

"Absolutely certain." Pippa grinned and then realized Logan was watching. "You're wondering why I'm happy about a delay?"

A lift of his shoulder and he met her gaze. "I never ask a woman what she's thinking."

Chapter Three

Logan waited for her smile and was rewarded by laughter instead. "So," Pippa said as she swept an errant strand of hair back over her ear, "how exactly does a guy make the career change from missionary to carpenter?"

"Involuntarily" slipped out of his mouth before he realized what he said.

That got her attention. Logan stifled a groan as he waited for the barrage of questions that usually came along with any admission of what he had once done and what now occupied his days.

"Yes, I suppose that happens, doesn't it? But then the Lord tells us our plans won't always be His," she said instead.

How many times had he heard that one? Or the statement about how everything happened for a reason? That one usually had him wanting to demand just what reason a loving God might have for taking the life of a woman whose only crime had been to listen to him when he insisted that she be on the flight that day.

Of course, he'd never actually said those things or responded to any of the other comments of those who were so sure of God's good plans. Nor would he say them now.

Only a few of his closest friends, fellow widowers at the church's Starting Over group, had heard any of them.

"Granny says your missions work has to do with kids."

Logan thought of the orphanage, of the little ones and teenagers he hadn't seen in more than three years. Some would be grown by now, others likely unrecognizable from the babies and toddlers they once were. "Yes, it did."

"Did? As in the past, then?"

Logan recalled the planes he and his wife had ridden, skimming the treetops before dropping down for a landing that almost instantly had them surrounded by happy and eager young faces. Resolutely he pushed away the image. "Yes."

Pippa turned to face the beach and then lifted her hand to shade her eyes. "Oh?" she said almost as an afterthought. "Would it be prying to ask why you're not involved in anything like that now?"

It would, but he told her anyway. "I've got obligations in Vine Beach to see to first."

She glanced over her shoulder to meet his gaze. "And then what will you do?"

Go back to Zambia. That's where he'd left his heart. And yet the longer he was away, the less he felt the Lord leading him back.

The truth was, for the first time since he gave his life to Christ, Logan had no idea what God wanted him to do after his late wife's property was sold and the money distributed. So until He gave other instructions, Logan intended to put all his effort into making that sale happen.

Pippa must have sensed he had no answer, or perhaps she realized he did not want to reply. Whatever the reason, she offered a wry smile and then nodded toward the spot where the satellite dish lay askew. "So, tell me more about your thoughts on a covering for the deck portion of the roof. Is that possible up there or would the wind make a structure like that a bad idea?"

And so it went, a smooth transition from the uncomfortable to the comfortable. Only later when Logan had deposited Pippa at her grandmother's doorstep did he wonder if she had managed that transition on purpose or by accident.

"Thank you for taking the time to show me your idea," she said as she climbed from the Jeep, her hand still on the door handle. "You probably noticed I like it very much."

And I like you.

The words came so close to the tip of his tongue that he actually bit down on his lower lip to keep from speaking. He glanced beyond her to where several people were loading catering equipment into the back of a Pop's Seafood Shack truck.

"Thank you for missing out on the party to come along and see it firsthand."

Her laughter caught his attention. The wind had whipped strands of her very proper do into a more casual style. In the waning light from the afternoon sun, Pippa Gallagher looked absolutely stunning. When she smiled and offered a goodbye, Logan found himself wishing he could stay just a few minutes longer.

"So I'll see you at the meeting next week," she said as she closed the door.

"Wednesday morning. Ten sharp," Logan said through the open window. "And I'll have the preliminary sketches to you by Monday afternoon."

Pippa rested her hand on the car door and leaned slightly forward to meet his gaze. "I would hate to be responsible for making anyone work on what is supposed to be a beautiful spring weekend."

Logan shrugged. "Nothing better to do."

"No?" she said. "You don't happen to skateboard, do you?"

"Nope. I prefer to keep my adventure to the water." At her confused look, he said, "Surfing."

"Oh. Well, surfing and skateboarding aren't much different. You balance on a board either way." Pippa tucked a golden strand behind her ear and, for the first time, he noticed she wore tiny pearl earrings.

"Different enough."

Logan thought of the surfboard he was working on in his garage, the one he'd probably sell as soon as the property issue was settled. If he worked quickly enough and the weather cooperated, he might get a few decent days of surfing from it before it was gone.

"You sure you don't want to give it a try? I've got this thing Saturday and I…" Pippa shook her head. "Your expression speaks for itself."

"Does it?"

A nod. "You're frowning, Logan."

"Oh, well…" He forced a smile. "How's that?" he said while trying to keep his grin in place.

"Worse." A warm wind ruffled the palms standing sentry on either side of the gate. "However, since you ignored my little incident with the umbrella, I'll pretend otherwise."

He patted his front pocket where the second paper umbrella still resided, and Pippa laughed. In the distance, a gull shrieked. She looked up to spy the white bird circle and then dive out of sight behind the house.

"Thanks for saving me from the speeches," Pippa said when she turned back toward Logan. She seemed to study him for a moment.

"I get points for that, right?" he called.

"Yes, but you lose them for not being brave enough to try a skateboard." She gave him a suspicious look. "Or have you changed your mind?"

Logan shifted the Jeep into Reverse. "Never."

And yet as he drove away, Logan couldn't help thinking if anyone could convince him to get on a skateboard, it would be Pippa Gallagher.

"Pippa, darling?"

Taking the phone off speaker, Pippa rose to close the door to the storage-closet-sized office she had claimed for her own at the skate park. Outside, the afternoon shadows were lengthening, but with the first-ever skating competition being held Saturday, there were too many details yet to handle.

Since Pippa had been forced to stay, she allowed those few kids who had nowhere else to go on a Tuesday night to stay, as well. They were now having a grand time on the ramps while she struggled to hear her grandmother. The door muffled the noise to an acceptable level.

"Yes, Granny. Sorry, I'm at the park and the kids are making noise. Are you back from visiting Aunt Betsy?" She returned to the squeaky chair and ancient metal desk that the previous owners had left.

"Why are you at the skate park so late?"

"Just tying up some loose ends. The outreach is Saturday, although the kids would rather call it a skating competition." Pippa leaned back and rested her head against the cinder block wall. "Anyway, everything all right with Aunt Betsy?"

"Everything is wonderful," she said. "I'm having such a great time that I've decided to stay here in Dallas an extra week. I hope you don't mind."

"Mind? No, of course not."

"Will you let our contractor know? His is the only appointment I've not yet canceled. I thought perhaps you could tell him yourself, what with the familiarity I saw between you at the reception last Saturday." A well-timed pause. "Interesting that the two of you left at exactly the same time. The speeches had barely begun."

There it was. The reprimand she expected. Or at least the beginning of it.

"Yes, Granny, about that. I do apologize."

"Do you?" Before Pippa could respond, Granny continued. "Well, we can discuss that when I return. Will you just please let our Logan know we're rescheduling?"

"I will," she said. "Would you like me to have him email the plans to you so you can look at them before next week?"

"Oh, goodness no. I've got a great-grandbaby to play with. Why in the world would I want to look at construction drawings? And besides, I prefer old-fashioned blueprints I can touch to some silly nonsense on a computer screen."

"Then I'll have him overnight the blueprints. That way you can study them."

"Have you not heard a word I've been saying, Pippa? Just handle things until I get back. Make all the decisions you want. It's going to be your home."

"And your gallery," Pippa reminded her.

"Yes, of course," Granny said, "but Gallagher and Company is hardly the reason for this renovation. It's just a very nice benefit of the project."

"Oh? What is the reason if not to build a gallery for your art?"

"Sorry, darling. I really must go. Bye now."

And then she was gone.

Pippa opened her laptop and sent a quick email to

Logan canceling tomorrow's meeting and rescheduling for the following Wednesday, then went back to putting together the skating competition.

A half hour later, she closed her computer, tucked it into her bag, then turned off the lights and locked the office. "Time to go," she called to the three skaters who remained. And then, "Anyone need a ride?"

They all did, of course, but asking them was a formality she allowed, as was the stop she made at the Hamburger Hut. At least she would know these three got home safely and had a large if not completely healthy meal.

"Invite everyone to the competition," she said as she turned down the street where all three lived.

"What if you can't pay?" the youngest of the group asked.

"Not a problem," Pippa said. "Anybody who can't come up with the entry fee can do some work for me around the skate park to earn the money."

That perked up all three, and soon they were chattering about decks and wheels and other skating essentials. When Pippa had dropped off the last of the trio at his door, she was still smiling.

If every kid had to work off his fee, she would still hold the event. The Lord would provide. It was just that simple.

Her route back to the rented cabin took Pippa past the building where she would soon be living. The windows were dark, indicating the work for today had ceased. A few minutes later she arrived home. The sound of the waves breaking against the shore filled her ears as Pippa grabbed her bag and headed up the stairs to the front door. Pausing on the deck, she placed her bag at her feet and then walked over to the rail to look out at the ocean.

The sun had dipped close to the horizon, but there was

still plenty of daylight left. To her right, the wide sweep of beach ended at the marina where sailboats rocked at anchor. On the left, the neon lights of Pop's Seafood Shack twinkled in the distance. In between, the sand shimmered as the water lapped at the beach and then quickly retreated.

Pippa inhaled deeply of the fresh salt air and then let her breath out slowly. Of all the things she missed about her life prior to coming to work for Granny, living in the city was not among them. Nor was the lack of fresh seafood or the ability to take a long run down the beach whenever she wanted.

And right now she decided that's exactly what she wanted.

Ten minutes later, Pippa had changed clothes and laced up her running shoes. She headed toward the marina at a slow pace, picking up speed as she neared the docks, and then turned around and retraced her steps toward the cabin. Instead of stopping, she kept going in the direction of Pop's Seafood Shack. If Leah was there, perhaps her friend would have time to share a slice of pie back in the kitchen. If not, then a piece of pie to go would do the trick.

Pippa took her customary route up the back stairs and into the kitchen with renewed vigor. It had been too long since she paid Leah a visit here. Unfortunately her friend was out.

"Leah's taking the night off," the cook told her. "You want the usual?"

"No catfish for me tonight," she said. "But I would like a slice of apple pie to go, if it's not too much trouble."

A few minutes later, she paid for the pie and headed back down the stairs. She had almost reached the deck when someone called her name.

Logan. She turned to face her building contractor. He, too, appeared to be carrying a slice of pie.

"Great minds think alike," he quipped as he closed the distance between them. "Did you come for the pie, too?"

"I had hoped for conversation and pie, but Leah's not here." Pippa nodded toward the take-out container in her hand. "So it's just pie."

"Want some conversation to go with it?"

"Sure," she said as she followed him over to the deck. "I wasn't expecting anyone but Leah to see me, so please excuse my choice of outfit."

He laughed. "I just figured you had decided to run off your meal before you ate it."

Logan settled at the edge of the deck, his feet in the sand, and Pippa joined him. Instantly several seagulls went on alert, hovering overhead and then coming to roost on the rail nearby. Pippa ignored them, just as she did every morning when she drank her coffee on the cabin's front porch, and dug her heels into the sand.

"You know, maybe there is something to this running first and eating pie later philosophy," Logan said as he reached for the plastic fork inside the container.

"Maybe so." They fell into companionable silence until Pippa decided to ask a question that had been bothering her. "So, Logan, you said something at my grandmother's party that has me confused."

He glanced at her. "What's that?"

"You said something about seeing kids up to no good. What did you mean by that?"

His attention went to the fork in his hand. Slowly he set it aside and then regarded Pippa with a serious look. "I'm not completely sure what you're asking."

"Well," she said slowly, "since I work with kids who aren't always considered socially acceptable, I'm wondering whether you were making that determination about the kids based on how they looked."

Logan seemed to consider the question a moment. Then he shrugged. "Partly. I think. If I remember right, the rest of what I said was that they reminded me of myself at that age." Logan reached for the fork again and then seemed to think better of it. "I wasn't exactly socially acceptable, either."

"I see."

"You sound disappointed in me."

In a way, she was. She let her silence speak for her.

"Look," he said gently. "I saw a lot of things in Africa what weren't pleasant, but what I did see was the family unit taking care of its own. We've lost that here. Kids roam the street and there's little anyone can do. Or maybe little they will do. At least until the kids have gotten in enough trouble for the authorities to intervene. I would like to stop that cycle."

"So would I." Pippa warmed to the topic. "That's why I'm so passionate about the skating outreach. These kids are outcasts, or at least they look like it, and they need a place to go so they're off the streets."

"I don't think that would have worked for me, so I'm not sure I can agree with your method."

"I see." She took a deep breath and let it out slowly. "And what would you suggest?"

"Rules, for a start. Some sort of order in their lives. Maybe a good talking-to or at least some incentive to stop hanging around doing nothing. I guess you could say I advocate a more direct approach between outcast and productive member of society."

Oh.

Pippa opened her mouth to argue and then decided taking a bite of pie was the better course of action. Obviously Logan's opinions and hers were in direct opposition.

He met her gaze. The man was attractive, even if he was completely wrong about the best way to win wayward souls to the Lord. "You don't like my approach."

"It doesn't matter whether I like it," she said. "I will say I disagree."

Logan nodded. "All right. But you need to understand I'm thinking about what's best for these kids. And considering I was one of them, I think I know what I'm talking about."

He was wrong, of course, but for the sake of continuing the discussion, she decided to attempt a different argument. "All right, just one more thing." Pippa mustered a smile. "I'm ready to prove you wrong."

"Are you, now?" Logan seemed to think on that. "Considering we're both wanting the same result for these kids, I hope you're right. In the meantime, I'll leave the skating to you and I'll stick to building construction."

This time her smile was genuine. "It's a deal. Though you have an open invitation to come and see what we're doing down there."

Logan closed the pie container, his dessert now gone. "I'll consider it," he said. "Now what say I walk you home?"

She rose to toss the remains of her pie into the trash can nearby. "Thanks, but after eating this, I probably ought to run back, too." Pippa smiled once more. "Oh, and consider this a formal invitation to come skate with me. Meet me at the building on Saturday at eight-thirty and we'll drive over together."

Pippa turned and headed off toward her cabin at a slow jog before he could respond.

"Hey," Logan called. "I never said I was coming. I just said I was thinking about it!"

Pippa picked up her pace and didn't look back until she reached the cabin. As she climbed the stairs, she glanced at the restaurant to see that Logan was still standing on the beach.

A moment later, her phone rang. Logan.

"Wondering what to wear?" she asked.

His laughter was deep and swift. "Hardly. I was wondering if I could strike a deal."

She leaned against the deck rail. "What kind of deal is that?"

"I'll skate with you if you'll surf with me."

"So skating on Saturday?"

"Not going to commit to that just yet." He paused. "But only because I've got a contractor who's been ditching me and I need to get him pinned down to a time he'll be available. If it's Saturday, then I won't be there."

"All right," Pippa said. "Now, as to what to wear—I'd say any of your baggy jeans and hooded sweatshirts will work just fine."

Logan was still laughing when she said goodbye.

Chapter Four

On Friday, Logan's usual construction update arrived along with a spreadsheet that detailed expenses, workers' time sheets, and other items pertinent to the project. Though Pippa was at the skate park, she opened the email and read the information it contained.

Finding everything in order, Pippa jotted off a note of thanks along with a reminder about tomorrow's skating event. With a smile, she hit Send. To her surprise, Logan called her almost immediately.

"You're not canceling on me," she said in lieu of a proper greeting.

"I just wanted to ask if I needed anything besides my life insurance policy. Oh, and I'll be sure to bring my medical insurance card, too."

Pippa laughed. "I've got all the things you'll need. Just—"

"Hey, I'm really sorry but I'm getting a call and I need to answer it. It's the subcontractor I told you about who's been ditching me lately, and I'd hate to miss him. I'll call you when we're done."

Pippa said goodbye and set the phone down. She

glanced up to see Rico Galvan, the artist who had painted her boots, standing at the door.

"Busy?"

"Come in," she said. "I'm just going over the check-list for tomorrow."

The teenager grinned and stepped inside, his paint-splattered coveralls telling where he'd been. For the past week, Logan had employed Rico to do demolition work, the dirty kind that removed the old in preparation for the new.

Rico had asked that Pippa not mention their association or his background at the skate ministry, and she had complied. He wanted to get the job on his own merits, something she understood completely.

"How's the job coming along?" Pippa asked.

"It's hard work, but I stay busy, and I like that." He paused. "So, I wondered if maybe…"

"I might have the Bibles here?" She nodded to the oversize box next to Rico's feet. "The delivery driver dropped them off a half hour ago."

His face shone. "Do you think I could take a look?"

"Actually," she said as she retrieved the scissors and walked toward him, "I hadn't planned to open the box until we could see them together." She handed him the scissors. "Here, Rico. You do the honors."

Made specially for the skating outreach and competition, these copies of the New Testament bore a cover created to look like the graffiti designs that Rico had painted on the outside of the skate park. A skater's Bible, one Pippa hoped she could someday afford to reprint and continue to give out as part of the ministry. Thanks to Leah and Ryan's donation, they would have enough for tomorrow, and that's what counted for now.

Rico made quick work of opening the box and then

moved the brown paper aside to reveal a stack of copies. A low whistle was his only response. And then he reached in and took one out, cradling it first in his palm and then against his chest.

When he looked up, his eyes glistened with tears. "I can't believe it."

Pippa reached to hug him and then stepped back. "I'm very proud of them. And of you."

The quiet young man could only nod.

"I'll see you tomorrow morning, then. Nine o'clock?"

Struggling to keep his emotions in check, Rico choked out a quick reply and turned to leave. Pippa watched him go. She was still watching him when her cell phone rang, drawing her back to her desk.

"I'm sorry I had to hang up so quickly." Logan gave her a brief description of his call with the subcontractor and then paused. "Pippa, about tomorrow...I'm going to have to take a rain check."

Pippa let out the breath she hadn't realized she was holding. "Oh?"

"This subcontractor's the best in the business when it comes to restoring old brick, and your building needs a lot of work. He's agreed to do it, but only if I meet him tomorrow to go over the specifics and supervise his guys."

"I understand," she said as she felt a small measure of relief. "And yes, you can definitely have a rain check."

"You could always drop by and say hello. If the job entails what I think it does, it's going to take most of the day."

She paused only a second. "I can't promise but I will see what I can do."

"Oh?" Logan laughed. "That was fast. I only just canceled and you've already got plans."

"Actually, *we* had plans. I was going to get you on a skateboard, remember?"

"Well," he said slowly, "you were going to try."

"Oh no, mister," Pippa said with mock seriousness. "If I can get out there with the kids, then I expect you to do the same. I thought you understood that I was inviting you to an outreach and not just for the two of us to skate. Remember, I told you I would show you that you were wrong. I can't do that without showing you what we do, now, can I?"

"I guess not. So our plans were to skate with kids?" Logan paused as the sound of hammering began. "Sorry, just stepped inside and it's loud in here. Hold on a sec." A door opened and then closed, and the hammering instantly ceased. "All right. Now, start over. I'm confused."

"The outreach ministry where I volunteer is having an event tomorrow. The kids are calling it a skating competition, but I prefer to think of it as an opportunity to hand out specially designed Bibles that match our graffiti logo. And to skate, of course."

"Of course."

She couldn't miss the less than enthusiastic tone in his voice. "Something wrong, Logan?"

Silence.

"Logan?"

"Yeah, I'm here," he said. "Look, I know this ministry means something to you. I mean, it must for you to volunteer your time. But I drove by there yesterday. It's the warehouse over on State Street, right? The one covered in gang graffiti?"

She didn't like his tone or his insinuation. "That's street art, and it's our logo. Taken from Romans 10:14." *And painted by your employee, Rico,* she longed to add. "Why?"

"I'm sorry to hear that, Pippa. The warehouse is hurting the value of the neighborhood. Do you have plans to cover that 'street art' any time soon?"

Well, that did it. Still, she kept her cool. After all, this was the man she had hired to turn Granny's dreams into reality. For all she wished to tell him about his opinions of Rico's art, her need to do so was tempered by the fact that Granny had the greatest respect for Logan.

"The art stays," she said. "And I hardly see how anything could bring down the value of that neighborhood. Other than the abandoned machine shop next door, the rest of the block is filled with empty lots and buildings that are in dire need of being torn down."

"Exactly," Logan answered, "and that's just what the guys from Starting Over are doing in a few weeks. Tearing down the dangerous buildings that the city owns but can't afford to pay to have demolished and painting over the ones that need work."

"That's great," she said. "I'm sure some of the kids would like to help with the cleanup. If I can get permission from their parents, that is. But the logo stays."

Silence.

"Logan?"

"I'm here."

She leaned back against the chair and let out a long breath. "Look, I thought we agreed to disagree."

"We did," he said evenly. "But this is different. That machine shop next door?"

"Yes."

"I'm the one trying to sell it, Pippa. And that's not going to happen as long as any potential buyers think the shop sits next to a gang hideout."

"That's ridiculous," she snapped.

"Well, maybe so, but I guess that's just one more thing

we will have to agree to disagree about. And should you change your mind…"

"Go on," she said instead of snapping back at him.

"Well," he said in a surprisingly kind tone. "I understand that to the kids this is art. Or rather street art. I really do. But please understand what I'm saying, too. The For Sale sign has been up over a month and I've only had one person inquire. Nobody wants to buy property in the wrong neighborhood. And—"

"And you think we give that impression." When he said nothing, Pippa felt compelled to continue. "I disagree, Logan. However, I would love to help any way I can with the cleanup. Who is in charge?"

"That would be me."

"Oh." Pippa forced a hopeful tone into her voice. "Well, good. Then count me in. I'll bring friends. The more the merrier, right?"

She couldn't help thinking as she hung up that Logan's enthusiasm was sorely missing. Well, no matter. She and the R10:14 kids would do their part to clean up their neighborhood. Then Logan would see the value in what happened behind the brightly painted exterior walls.

Chapter Five

The last of the skaters left R10:14 a little after three on Saturday afternoon. Pippa tossed the bags into the trash bin and then walked back over to be certain the warehouse doors were securely locked. The day had been long, but thanks to the loan of an industrial-sized fan, the skaters had kept cool.

The first-ever Vine Beach skating competition had brought out several dozen kids from as far away as Galveston, and many of them were new to R10:14. And though the prizes were modest, none of the winners complained when he or she was awarded a T-shirt.

More important, each entrant received a copy of the New Testament bound in a trendy graffiti print courtesy of Rico and his tagging skills. The words of Romans 10:14, the ministry's signature verse, were scrawled across the front cover in a brilliant hue:

How, then, can they call on the one they have not believed in? And how can they believe in the one of whom they have not heard? And how can they hear without someone preaching to them?

Pippa counted it a victory that only three skaters left their copies behind. She prayed over each one of the three, asking God to send those teenagers back and cause them to bring friends along with them. She added a prayer that somehow the Lord would soften Logan's heart and help him to see the kids and the ministry the way she did.

Pippa climbed into her car and turned the key, bristling at the thought that a good man like Logan Burkett couldn't see beyond the street art outside to the good things going on inside. As the Mini Cooper's air-conditioning filled the space, she let out a long breath and forced her temper to cool, as well. She would win him over. After all, Logan wasn't a bad guy. He just had a different way of looking at things.

"You're in control, God," she whispered.

Pippa reached into her bag to retrieve the copy Rico had proudly given her and traced each letter, thinking of how far the former juvenile delinquent had come. A tap on her window made Pippa jump and the book tumbled to the floor.

When Pippa lowered the window, Riley Burkett was quick to apologize. "I didn't mean to frighten you," he said. "I saw you were here and thought I'd say hello." His gaze fell to the book on the floor mat. "What's that?"

"It's Rico's New Testament." She leaned to retrieve it, then handed the copy to Logan's father. "He did the artwork himself, and a donation from Leah and Ryan over at Pop's Seafood allowed us to have plenty of copies printed up for the competition this weekend. I'm quite proud of him."

"As well you should be," the older man said as he opened the book and smiled. "Seems like yesterday I was having to report Rico once or twice a week for tagging my vacant properties, and now he's using his artistic talent for something like this?" His gaze met hers. "This is incredible."

Pippa smiled. Both knew the story of the eighteen-year-old who could just as easily have turned to a life of crime rather than a life led for the Lord. Thanks to Riley Burkett's recommendation, Rico had been doing maintenance work and other odd jobs for Burkett Properties in addition to the demo job for Logan.

"Yes, it is beautiful, isn't it?" Pippa smiled. "Rico is applying to colleges. Did you know that?"

Mr. Burkett shook his head. "I didn't, but you tell that young man if he needs a reference letter, I'd be happy to write one."

Her heart soared. "He will be thrilled."

"It would be my pleasure," he said as he handed the Bible back to her.

"No, keep it," Pippa told him. "I know he would want you to."

The Realtor tucked the book under his arm and grinned. "Thank you." His expression sobered. "I've got to admit to an ulterior motive in stopping by."

"Oh?"

"I felt like I should warn you." Mr. Burkett glanced around and then leaned toward her. "About the kids using the parking lot."

"There's been a complaint," she supplied.

His look of discomfort spoke for him. "Nothing formal, but the owner feels…"

Pippa sighed. "The kids are bringing down the value of the neighborhood and keeping the property from selling. Yes, Logan told me."

Mr. Burkett's nod was brief. "I've tried to explain to him that in this market it is not unusual for a property such as the machine shop to go without an offer for many, many months."

Pippa thought of the lease on the warehouse and how inexpensive the rent had been for that very reason. An ideal solution would be to buy both buildings and achieve the dual purpose of gaining an outdoor space for her skaters and losing a neighbor bent on complaining.

Unfortunately there was no room in her budget—or Granny's—for such an expense. Perhaps someday, but definitely not until the Branson Building was completed and the gallery open and turning a profit.

"I'm determined to show Logan he's wrong," Pippa said. "I've challenged him to come by and see what we do."

"My son may not realize it just yet, but I'm well aware of what a great job you're doing." Mr. Burkett glanced over his shoulder and seemed to be studying the warehouse. "Your grandmother tells me you'll be running the gallery when it opens. What will you do with this place then?"

"My goal is to divide my time between both."

"An ambitious plan." He shrugged. "But who am I to say it can't be done?"

Pippa grinned. "Exactly."

"I would say the same about your project to win Logan over. You'll let me know how I can help with that, won't you?"

"Of course."

"Then I'll look forward to hearing from you." Mr. Burkett winked. "And in the meantime, I'll work on that stubborn son of mine. Maybe see if I can get him to come for supper. Speaking of supper, my wife will not be happy if I forget to pick up cornmeal."

Pippa joined him in laughing. "Thank you for saying hello," she said as they parted ways. "And don't worry about Logan. He'll come around."

Mr. Burkett waved as he climbed into his car. "I was just about to say that," he called before he started the engine and drove away.

Pippa did the same, aiming her car toward downtown Vine Beach. What better time to begin her campaign to get Logan's support than right now? And he had invited her to stop in and view the construction progress.

Unfortunately, when Pippa reached the Branson Building, she found everything locked up and no evidence anyone was still there. *Lord, give me an opportunity to change his mind very soon, won't You?* Just to be sure, she pulled to a stop in front of the building and then called Logan.

He picked up on the second ring. "I was just thinking of calling you."

She hadn't expected that. "Oh?"

"Yes, but you called me. So, what's up?"

Pippa leaned back against the seat and shifted the phone to the other ear. "I told you I would stop by the building. I just wanted to be sure you weren't still there."

"Actually I'm down at the marina."

That explained the screeching of gulls on the other end of the line. "That answers my question. I won't keep you, then."

"No, wait. I was about to take Eric's boat out. Want to join me?"

Pippa caught sight of herself in the rearview mirror. The day had been long, and every minute of it showed on her face. But this was Logan. Her building contractor.

And she *had* asked the Lord to give her an opportunity to change his mind. Indeed this qualified as "very soon."

"Remember I've been at the outreach all day," Pippa warned.

"Then a sail around the bay, a swim and a picnic on Sand Island sound like exactly what you need."

It did.

"Sure," she said. "I'll be there in ten minutes. I just need to stop by the cabin and change clothes."

It took just a few minutes to reach the cabin. Pippa changed into her yellow swimsuit, tossed on shorts and a T-shirt and then grabbed a towel. Logan was waiting for her on deck, his smile broad as she walked toward Eric's sailboat.

"Right on time," he said.

Pippa checked her phone and then tossed it into the bag with her towel. "Ten minutes exactly. So, how did you manage to appropriate Eric's boat?"

"Between his veterinary practice and the kids, he and Amy don't get out on the water much anymore. He's too stubborn to sell the boat, but he doesn't mind loaning it out to his stepbrother to do a little preventative maintenance trip every once in a while."

She allowed him to help her on board. "I see."

His hand lingered a moment against her back as he steadied her. "Ready?"

"Definitely." Stowing her bag, Pippa watched as Logan untied the rope and then steered the sailboat out to open water. "What a beautiful afternoon."

Whether Logan heard, she couldn't tell. He seemed too intent on his duties as ship's captain to notice anything beyond the water, the wind and their course across the bay. They sailed against the tide, slicing through the waves with ease. Pippa settled back to enjoy the ride while Logan attended to his duties.

After a while, he set anchor some twenty yards from Sand Island, the uninhabited stretch of sand in the center of Vine Beach Bay that was a favorite spot for picnics and shell collecting. "Hungry yet?"

She was. "Oh, I should have brought something."

"No need." Logan reached into the galley and produced a cooler. "I'm prepared to share." He met her gaze, his expression gleeful. "Unless you don't like hot dogs cooked over an open fire and s'mores for dessert."

While Pippa couldn't remember the last time she'd had a hot dog, the s'mores sounded wonderful. "Perfect."

Logan tied a rope to the cooler and lowered it down into the water. "There's another cooler just over there," he said, pointing behind her. "My towel's already in there with the things we'll need to have a picnic. Why don't you put yours in it and then bring it to me? We can float over to the island with the coolers."

She did as he asked and then handed him the cooler. "Ladies first," he said, indicating that she should jump into the water.

Pippa dove in and then bobbed to the surface, exhilarated by the warm water. "Oh, this feels great," she said as she swam over to grasp the cooler full of towels while Logan executed a perfect dive. A moment later, he appeared and shook the water from his hair.

Grasping the rope on the cooler, he paddled toward Sand Island. Pippa followed a few yards behind, preferring to allow the current to float her to shore with the cooler. Drying off, she spread the towels out on the sand while Logan gathered sticks. Before long, Logan had a small fire going.

"Anything new to report on the building progress?" she asked as she held her hot dog stick over the fire and watched it begin to roast.

"Nothing major, though we got a lot of little things done today, and those add up." Logan removed his hot dog and placed it in a bun, then did the same for Pippa. "I've got a great guy working for me doing the demolition, so that makes a difference."

Pippa casually smoothed mustard onto her hot dog. "Rico?"

His eyebrows shot up. "Yeah, that's the guy. Rico Galvan. Know him?"

"I do, actually, and I like him very much." Only her promise to keep silent on her connection to the teenager kept her from saying anything further.

"I could use several more just like him."

"And I know just where you can find them," she said sweetly as she took a bite of the hot dog. "This is good," she managed after she finished the bite. "I haven't had hot dogs cooked outdoors like this in ages."

Logan shook his head. "No, you don't. You're not going to make a statement like that and then change the subject. By saying you know where I can find more guys like Rico, I'm guessing you're talking about your skater kids."

She met his gaze. The man did have the most beautiful eyes. "I am."

"Thanks, but I'll pass," Logan said.

"Because you don't believe kids can look like mine do and work like Rico does?"

Her companion took a bite of his hot dog and then leaned back on one elbow. He remained silent until he had finished. "Want another?"

"Thanks, but no. I'm waiting for my dessert."

Logan speared another hot dog and then held it over the flame. "I don't like how that sounds," he said.

"How what sounds?"

He gave her a sideways look. "What you said about not believing you." Before Pippa could respond, Logan held up his hand to silence her. "But it's true. What you said is accurate."

Not what she expected. Pippa watched as Logan completed the cooking and set about finishing his hot dog. Just when she thought he would say nothing further on the topic, Logan once again captured her gaze.

"I think I need a mulligan," he said.

"A mulligan?"

"It's a golf term for a do-over." He leaned forward. "I need to learn that just because a kid looks like I did, it doesn't mean he's going to turn out like me."

Pippa shrugged. "I don't think you turned out so terrible," she said gently.

"Oh, you missed the part where I went from horrible to…well…to whatever you'd call this."

Handsome. Funny. A guy who caught her attention when he stepped into the room. *Someone I'd like to know a little better.*

Pippa shook off the thought and opted for a diversion instead. "I'd call you ready for dessert," she said as she reached into the cooler to grab the package of marshmallows. "Shall I do the honors?"

"Please." He was smiling. It was almost as if he'd read her thoughts. Which of course was ridiculous.

Later, after they had eaten the gooey chocolate desserts, Logan tucked the remains of their picnic into the cooler and then doused the fire. Covering up the embers with sand, he sat back on the towel and looked off into the distance.

"You know, Pippa," he said slowly, "I appreciate that you don't mind challenging me."

She turned to face him. "I don't know what you mean."

"You're the only one I know who can turn my thoughts around without preaching or lecturing."

An indication that the Lord was hearing her prayers. And answering. "If you've changed your mind about anything, it's not coming from me."

"Fair enough, but you're the one delivering the message."

"Does that mean you'll give my skaters a chance?"

"That means I'll do better about not judging on appearances." Logan paused to swipe at the sand on his leg. "If you're still willing to put a team together, I'd be happy to add them to the list for the neighborhood cleanup."

"Thank you, Logan," Pippa said.

He returned his attention to her, his expression thoughtful. "Now, about your warehouse. What color would you like our guys to use when they paint over the graffiti?"

Her eyes narrowed. "Logan…"

His serious expression dissolved as laughter bubbled forth. "I'm kidding, Pippa. Unless you'd like us to paint it for you."

She gave him a playful jab.

"I'll take that as a no, at least for now." Logan nodded toward the water. "The waves aren't big enough to surf, so how about a swim? Or are you ready to head back?"

"A swim would be great."

And it was, as was the sail back to the marina a little later. They arrived just as the sun dipped low over the horizon, casting long purple shadows along the shore.

Pippa helped Logan secure the sailboat and then walked back with him toward the parking lot. He tucked her bag into the trunk and then stepped back to watch her open the car door. Just before she climbed inside, he placed his hand on hers.

"I had a wonderful time," he said.

"So did I. Thank you for the invitation."

"Thank you for accepting." He took a step back. "Guess I'll see you on the job site next week sometime."

"And at the meeting with Granny on Wednesday," she reminded him as she started the car.

They parted with a smile, and as Pippa glanced into her rearview mirror, she saw Logan silhouetted against the sunset. Slowly, he lifted one hand to wave and she returned the gesture.

Only when she dumped the contents of the bag onto the deck of her cabin a few minutes later did she realize she hadn't checked for calls or, for that matter, cared whether she'd talked to anyone while she enjoyed herself with Logan.

Thankfully she hadn't missed any summons from Granny or chances at conversation with Leah or Amy. Not that it would have mattered, she decided.

Time spent with Logan Burkett was worth missing any of those things. And now she knew she was in real trouble.

Chapter Six

Logan looked up from his work in time to see the text message scroll across the screen: Busy?

He was, though his father so rarely texted that the occasion warranted a response. He picked up the phone and a moment later heard his dad's voice on the line. "What's up?" he asked as he closed his laptop and swiveled around in his chair to face the window.

"Just had you on my mind," Riley said. "And I was wondering how things were coming along with the Gallagher ladies."

"Things are coming along great. I've got a meeting set up for Wednesday to get final approval on the plans. The kid you recommended for the demo work is a hard worker, so barring any unforeseen circumstances, I'd say the real construction work will start no later than next Monday. And I finally met with your brick guy this morning. Got the bid in and the preliminary work started."

"Glad to hear it, especially in regard to Rico. He's a good guy. I'm glad you're pleased with his work."

"I was skeptical," Logan said as he thought of the quiet teenager who had arrived early and stayed late. The kid

Pippa knew and liked. Thanks to him the project was already ahead of schedule. At this rate, Rico would be working himself out of a job in a few days. Maybe Logan would find something else for the kid to do just so he could keep him on the payroll.

"Well, in any case," Dad continued, "I'm glad it's working out. Now, about the machine shop."

Logan's hopes rose. "Has there been some interest in it?"

"Nothing new, but I think it's time to drop the price."

Logan frowned. "The money isn't mine to lose, Dad. I had really hoped to get close to the asking price. I owe it to her to get the most I can from it."

He owed his late wife so much more. Making the most from the investments Ashley left would have to suffice.

"I know, son," his father said gently, "but you've got to decide how long you want to wait. There's something to be said for making adjustments so that the property can sell." A pause. "Until that happens, you can't do a thing for the kids she wanted to help."

The truth, and he knew it. And yet he'd already waited far too long.

"Starting Over guys are staging a cleanup soon. Right now the abandoned buildings are an eyesore, but then so is Pippa's skating outreach. I've tried to convince her to remove that graffiti, but she refuses. She just can't see that it's bringing down the whole neighborhood."

"A neighborhood you completely ignored until recently."

"I wasn't ready."

"I'm not sure you're ready now," his father said. "Are you running from or to?"

A question the elder Burkett had asked a hundred times during Logan's growing-up years. If he'd been honest, Logan would have admitted most of the time he was running from.

After the accident, he'd busied himself with construction work that kept him as far as possible from Vine Beach and the memories. Only when Dad's ultimatum brought him home for Christmas and ultimately into the family business, albeit on a temporary basis, did he admit he'd been running from them too.

But now? He wished he could say for sure.

"Son? Which is it?"

He ran his hand through his hair and then gripped the phone tighter. "To, I think."

"To what?"

"A resolution," Logan said as he thought of his recent conversation with Pippa. "Or maybe just to a place where everything I did wrong is behind me and there's nothing else I have to apologize for. Then I can start fresh somewhere else."

"I see. Like Alaska?"

"I was fine there," Logan said, hating how defensive he sounded. The truth of the matter was that he'd been fine there only because no one knew him. He didn't have to explain why he was no longer a missionary. And why he was now a widower.

A pause. "Any other idea where that somewhere else might be?"

"Back to Africa maybe, or…" Logan leaned back and closed his eyes. "Or wherever I'm supposed to go. I figure I'll know when the time comes."

"And you're sure you're supposed to leave Vine Beach?"

He wasn't and yet everything in him demanded that he find a fresh start in a place where no one knew him as Logan the troubled teenager or, worse, as Logan the widower. He was both, or had been, but neither really covered who he was now.

Or rather who he wanted to be.

Then he had the odd thought that Pippa knew him as neither. She alone saw him as he was before he went off looking for trouble and then returned to his life once that trouble had been placed squarely behind him. She was an anomaly. More than that, she was someone he might have found more than a little interesting under other circumstances.

Logan opened his eyes and swiveled around to spy the yellow paper umbrella he'd tossed onto a stack of mail last week. Until now he hadn't noticed that the souvenir was the same color as Pippa Gallagher's swimsuit. He snatched it up and twirled the umbrella between two fingers.

"Look, Logan," Dad said in that tone he took on when a statement of disapproval was about to follow. "You've decided you're going to sell the shop. That's fine. But think about it, son. You want the money to help kids and yet you're complaining about kids who obviously need help. Don't you see the irony in that?"

"I'm not complaining about the kids."

"You're complaining about the place where they gather. That's the same thing, isn't it?" Dad paused. "Have you actually met any of them?"

"I've seen them," Logan said. "That was enough for me."

"Enough to decide you don't like them?" Riley asked.

Logan scrubbed at his face with his palm and then let out a long breath. "No, Dad," he said evenly. "It's not about liking them. It's about being concerned."

"Fair enough," his father said. "What are you concerned about?"

"Their futures, Dad. Have you seen them? When I look at them, I see kids who dress like thugs."

"You see yourself at that age," Riley interrupted. "And you were heading in the wrong direction then. I'm glad you're concerned about them, son. I really am. And I'm glad you're taking a stand. However, I wonder if you're correct in assuming that Pippa's way of reaching them isn't working."

Again Dad had stabbed directly into the heart of the truth. Logan had no immediate defense for the statement. "I didn't say that."

"But you're thinking it."

Logan let out a long breath. "Yes, I suppose I was. I know she hasn't been at this very long, but the kids look like troublemakers, and the place is painted like a gang hideout."

"I'll grant you that I wasn't thrilled, but there's nothing in their lease that says the building has to be painted a certain way." Dad paused. "And as to the kids, honestly, Logan, do you really think a change of clothes will make the difference?"

"It did with me."

"No," Dad said. "What made the difference with you was getting in trouble with the law and ending up in juvenile detention. Don't assume that others are as hardheaded as you were."

When Logan didn't immediately respond, his father continued. "The Bible says when there is a dispute, we are to go to the other person and work it out. Have you spoken to Pippa about this?"

Again the thought of Pippa and her yellow swimsuit rose in his mind. "I have."

"Well, good. I hope you two can see eye-to-eye. I like her very much."

"I doubt she'll change her mind," Logan said as he thought of their discussion on the topic. "In fact, she offered to help with the neighborhood cleanup day."

"I hope you agreed."

"Not willingly," he admitted, "but yes, I did."

"Logan," his dad said in a warning voice.

A ragged silence stretched between them. Outside the window, the oleander swayed in the breeze. Logan tossed the umbrella back on the stack of mail.

"Dad," he finally said, "I'm sorry. I didn't mean to start an argument."

"Nor did I," his father was quick to say.

Logan paused, determined not to end the call like this. He thought of his stepmother, Eric's mom, and from that came the idea for a change of topic. "Tell Susan if the offer is still open, I would love to join you and the rest of the family for Sunday games night."

"Is that so?"

Logan could hear the smile in his father's voice. He hadn't shown up for the Sunday night board game and potluck extravaganza at the Burkett home in months. Enduring a few hours of fun with his stepbrother and his family when he ought to be working was time well spent, and not just because it pleased Dad and Susan.

"Yes, Dad, that's so." Logan lifted the lid on his laptop and watched the screen light up. "Now let me get back to these blueprints so I can finish the changes or I just might have to miss tomorrow night after all."

"Oh no, you won't. See you tomorrow. Oh, and Logan?"

"Yes?"

"I hope you and Pippa enjoyed your sail."

Was anything private in a small town? "Yes, Dad, we did."

Logan couldn't miss his father's chuckle. Of course Dad would approve. After all, he and Pippa's grandmother were longtime friends.

"Will you be seeing her again, outside of the work you're doing for her at the Branson Building?" Dad asked.

"I am, actually." Logan let his father think on that statement for a moment and then added, "At the neighborhood cleanup."

"Have I mentioned how very much I like that girl?"

Logan shook his head. "Yes, you have. Now I really should get back to work."

"Yes, of course. But why don't you bring Pippa to games night? Susan would love to see her."

Sure, blame your matchmaking on your wife. "Bye, Dad."

His father was still chuckling when Logan hung up. As he went back to work on the drawings, he couldn't help smiling. If only they could agree on things that mattered. Like the eyesore she called a ministry location.

With Granny away, Pippa arrived at Gallagher and Company on Monday morning hoping to catch up on details that had eluded her last week. Though she had a perfectly good home office at the house on the beach, Pearl Gallagher had rented this space a few doors down from the Branson Building. Pippa Gallagher thought the expense extravagant. Granny, however, refused to hear any argument on the matter.

It was nice to actually go to an office rather than deal with the details of Granny's empire from a desk shoved into the corner of her studio-style beach house. And the view of downtown Vine Beach through the plate-glass windows served up a never-ending scene of small-town life that included the newspaper office, a small park and the one-story Vine Beach Courthouse. A huge contrast from the twenty-seventh-floor office she'd worked from in her last job.

Because it was a workday rather than one where she might actually be required to meet with Granny or any of her associates, Pippa had dressed casually in sandals, knee-length khaki shorts and a white top emblazoned with the Greek letters of her college sorority. A thin gold chain at her neck was her only attempt at accessorizing.

Settling at her desk, Pippa clicked through to the appropriate screen on the computer to pull up her email. Among the several dozen others, two caught her attention. Both were from Logan Burkett.

Upon opening the first one, she found the revised renovation plans as promised. The second one, sent only a few minutes ago, bore this cryptic question: Busy?

She looked up to see him wave from his spot on a bench across the street. With a grin, she typed back: Very. Another glance in his direction and she deleted the word and closed out her email program. Logan was her contractor, not some high school boy to flirt with.

Pippa could see him waiting even as she rose and stepped out of his line of sight to retrieve a coffee cup from the kitchenette in the back. When she returned to her desk, Logan was gone.

Disappointment rose immediately. And then came the chirp of her email alert. Logan.

Got a second? Need an opinion down at the job site if you're not too busy.

Pippa rose and returned to the kitchenette to transfer her coffee to the pretty Lily Pulitzer travel mug that was her favorite. Locking the office behind her, she made her way down the sidewalk to find the door to her future home open and Logan sitting comfortably on the stairs.

Dressed in cargo shorts and a cotton chambray shirt rolled up to show muscled forearms, Logan didn't look as if he belonged at a construction site. Only his paint-splattered work boots gave him away. When Pippa met Logan's gaze, she couldn't help noticing his broad smile.

"You look awfully sure that I would show up," she said as she watched the carpenter unfold his long legs and stand.

A shrug. "I had hoped to catch you before you got too busy." His gaze swept the length of her. "I see you're not dressed for any important events today."

"Working for Granny isn't all parties and fun."

He rested his arm on the stair rail. "No?"

"No, and believe it or not, the IRS does not care what you wear to work when you're preparing quarterly tax statements."

"I thought you were a party planner."

"Corporate events planner for an oil and gas firm in Dallas," she corrected. "But I started my business life in the tax accounting department. Got out of there as fast as I could, though. Now I just make sure Granny's CPA has all the information he needs to do his job." She looked down at her casual attire and then back up at Logan. "And sometimes I even get to wear shorts and sandals to work."

Logan made a show of looking down at her sandals. "Sandy feet and all?"

She hid her grin behind the coffee mug and then took a sip. "Absolutely. So," she said, "you had some questions?"

"I do." Logan nodded up the stairs. "I figure since you're going to be the one living in the apartment, you probably don't have to run the design decisions through your grandmother. Although if we need to wait until a day when she can be here, that's fine, too."

"No, that won't be necessary."

"If you've got the time, do you want to take a look at the samples for flooring and countertops? I've got paint color catalogues, too, if you're ready to make that decision."

"Sounds like fun." Pippa followed him up the stairs and into the loftlike space that would be her home someday soon.

The kitchen, not much bigger than the kitchenette at the office, was tucked into the corner of the second-floor space. This choice had been intentional, for Pippa was not much of a cook, though she recognized that she would need someplace to prepare simple meals.

Windows on two sides of the open space flooded the room with light and offered a sweeping view of downtown Vine Beach and its namesake seashore beyond. If she looked closely, Pippa could even see Sand Island, the minuscule picnic site situated a short boat ride off the coast.

"What do you think of these?" Logan nodded toward several catalogues of cabinet samples from major cabinetry manufacturers that were spread across an upended crate.

She reached for the nearest one and opened to the first page. The kitchen depicted there was lovely, as was the one on the next page. Thumbing through a few more examples, Pippa finally shook her head and set the catalogue aside.

"Something wrong?"

"These cabinets are all very nice, but what about the old cabinets I saw downstairs? Aren't they original to the building?"

"They are," he answered. "Why?"

Pippa shrugged. "Can't we make them work up here? I'd hate to spend money on new cabinetry when there are perfectly good ones downstairs. And actually I like them better than anything I see in here."

Logan gave her an admiring look. "Are you serious?"

"Absolutely." Pippa shrugged. "Why, don't you think it's a good idea?"

"I think it's a great idea, actually. I hated to think of what would happen to all that old wood."

She moved toward the window but kept her attention on Logan. "Well, there's the answer to that question. Now, what else do I need to decide?"

He gestured to the floor beneath her feet, a sadly neglected scuffed length of wide planks that were so dirty it was impossible to discern what type of wood they were. And yet Pippa wondered if a little cleaning and some repair would bring back their patina.

"What were you thinking?"

When she told him, Logan nodded thoughtfully. "A very good choice for this room, but we've got a bathroom to consider. I'm thinking wood's not going to work so well in there, what with this being a beach town."

"I suppose you're right. What do you suggest?"

Again he seemed to consider her question. "We haven't decided on countertops for the kitchen yet, so let me run something by you. There's a length of marble downstairs that was either part of the old kitchen or a display of some sort out front. There isn't much left, maybe eight or ten running feet, but it's in great shape and would make a nice floor for the bathroom or countertop in your kitchen."

Pippa lifted one eyebrow. "Show me."

She followed him back downstairs and then over a carefully cleared path that led into the former kitchen. Here the only reminder of the giant ovens that had once turned out Branson's bread and baked goods was the hooks on the wall where the cooking tools once hung.

Someone had made neat stacks of the wainscoting and wood trim that had been carefully removed from the space before the wall separating the front and back rooms was demolished. Beside the trim was a pile of metal squares.

"Ceiling tiles we're saving to use in the gallery," Logan explained as he moved past them to gesture toward a beautiful slab of white marble with a subtle gray vein running through it.

"Is this Carrara marble?" she asked.

"Could be," he said.

Pippa reached past Logan to trace the meandering pattern with her index finger. The stone was cool to her touch. To her surprise, not a smidge of dust lingered. Rico was certainly good at his job.

"It's lovely," she said as she took a half step back to get a better look. "I just can't decide whether to put it in the kitchen or the bath. If only there were more of this."

"Are you thinking you'd use it in both spaces if we could locate more?"

"Definitely. I can't imagine anything I would like better." Pippa looked up at Logan. "So I guess I'll have to rely on you to tell me where this would best fit."

He scratched his head. "Well, if you really wanted the same marble in both rooms, I'd say that's not going to happen. Not the exact same anyway. However, if you were willing to go with something that looked very much like it, maybe something that was reclaimed like this is, then I may be able to help."

"Really?"

"Really." He checked the stainless-steel watch on his wrist and then met her gaze. "I know this place. It's basically a salvage yard, but the owner comes up with all sorts of nice pieces. He just might have something. I was about to head over to the yard in Dad's truck. Want to ride along?"

She smiled. "What a great idea."

"After you, then," Logan said as he escorted Pippa outside and locked the door behind them. A few minutes later they were riding down the beach road with the waves lapping at the sand on their right and the prairie grass waving in the ocean breeze on their left.

"This is much more fun than working on quarterly income tax reports," she said over the sound of the wind and the waves.

"I should hope so," Logan said. "Although we're both going to have to pretend we're working or my guess is your grandmother will not be happy with us."

Pippa swiveled to get a better view of him. As he glanced quickly in her direction, she affected a serious expression. "I don't know about you, but I find this work to be exhausting."

His laughter filled the truck. "You and I are going to get along just fine."

As long as I don't mention R10:14.

Chapter Seven

Pippa rode in silence as all the familiar Vine Beach landmarks fell behind them. Growing up a missionary kid in Sumatra, she'd never quite gotten over the feeling of Texas sand between her toes. Once the treat she enjoyed when her parents took respite breaks from Indonesia and stayed with Granny, the waterfront's easy access still awed her.

Even during her high school years when Mom and Dad shipped her back to Texas to stay with her grandmother full-time, Pippa never believed it would be permanent. After all, nothing in a missionary's life ever felt that way, did it?

She was about to ask Logan that question when he slowed to signal a turn. "Are we here already?"

"Yes, ma'am." He offered a curt nod, then gestured to the only establishment on this stretch of highway. "This is the contractor's wonderland, also known as Curt's Salvage. But don't ask for Curt. He sold the place years ago to a guy named Dino. Dino sold it to his cousin Joe, who, last I heard, had retired and handed over the keys to his son, Joey."

"So Curt's Salvage is owned by some guy named Joey?"

Logan's grin was just the sort to cause a girl's heart

to flutter. If the girl was interested in handsome carpenters, that is. "Exactly," he responded.

Pippa resolutely turned her attention away from her sandy-haired companion to focus her attention on their destination. Bordered by a perimeter of weathered boards fashioned into a mismatched version of a picket fence, Curt's Salvage was a place so nondescript that she had been passing it for years and never noticed its existence.

Logan made his way across a gravel parking lot and pulled to a stop beside a pair of double doors that had been thrown open to the morning sun. Before he could climb out, Pippa had already bounded from the vehicle and was moving toward some French doors leaning against the wall just inside the building.

"What do you think?" she asked when he caught up to her. "For the bathroom, I mean. Wouldn't it be lovely to allow a little natural light in there?"

"I see your point," Logan said as he ran his hand over the aged wood and then pulled out one of the doors to inspect it. "But it's a bathroom. This won't allow for much privacy."

"I live alone, Logan," she reminded him. "And I was thinking of putting a sheer curtain behind it. Something to block the view but not the light."

"All right, but what about the other one? The sign says they come in a pair."

Pippa thought a moment and then shrugged. "I'm sure you'll figure out something."

His laughter trailed her as she made her way toward the next item that caught her attention. Curt's Salvage was a veritable treasure trove of castoffs, antiques and reclaimed items. Filled to the rafters, the place made her head spin. And as Pippa spied yet another great find, it made her heart thump.

By the time she'd walked the length of the building and the outdoor space behind it, she had found several more things she had to have. Logan did talk her out of buying the rusting red British phone box, which she'd wanted to use as a pantry, and an old pull-down schoolhouse map that she liked but had no use for.

"That was a profitable trip," Pippa said a short while later as she followed Logan out to the truck. "I didn't expect to find so many items for the loft."

"True, but it's a shame about the marble." Logan shook the sawdust out of his hair and closed the tailgate.

"Who would have thought someone would come along and buy out everything they had yesterday?" Pippa fitted the seat belt back into place and then glanced behind her at the treasures stashed in the back of the truck. "But we did find some great things. I had no idea this place was here."

"Hey, Logan!"

Pippa looked up to see a Willie Nelson look-alike in overalls and red bandanna bolting out the door at a much greater speed than a man of his age should have been able to manage. "Who's that?" she asked Logan.

"Hey, Joey. I didn't know you were here." Logan stepped out of the truck and then leaned in through the window. "That's—"

"The owner of Curt's?" She paused. "Figured so."

With a nod, Logan stepped away from the truck to envelop the older man in a hug. "Glad you didn't get away without me catching you," she heard Joey say. "I've got something special I set aside for you. Bring the little lady and come see."

Logan cast a tentative glance in her direction, his expression a question. Pippa responded with a shrug and then climbed out of the truck to follow the pair back inside Curt's Salvage.

She walked a step behind Logan as he made his way through the showroom, if the jumble of items stacked one upon the other could be called that, and then out a side door to stop in front of what appeared to be a small storage shed. Joey fumbled with a key chain filled with keys of all shapes and sizes until he found the one that opened the lock.

"Wait here," he said with a wink before disappearing inside.

Something clattered to the floor inside the shed, causing Pippa to jump.

"Are you all right, Joey?" Logan called.

"Yep, just fine. Now hang on a second while I…" Another crash, this time accompanied by what sounded like breaking glass.

Logan stepped forward to jerk open the door and nearly got hit by a slab of pale wood covered in dozens of fading and cracked stickers in neon colors. "Watch out there," Joey said as he leaned the wood against the wall of the shed.

"It's a longboard." The awe in Logan's voice told Pippa this was something special. Her eyes told her something else entirely. "A vintage Greg Noll."

"Sure is." The salvage shop owner stepped back to stand beside Logan. Both men remained silent. Almost awestruck.

Pippa crossed her arms over her chest and studied the surfboard. Nothing in what she saw gave away the reason for the two men's admiration. Perhaps with the stickers removed and a new coat of lacquer the board might look something akin to decent, but in its current condition it was truly pitiful.

"Exactly what makes this so special?" she asked.

The pair turned to stare, their expressions aghast. "It's a Greg Noll," Logan said. "I've heard about these but never seen one until now. How old do you think this one is?"

"Early sixties would be my guess," Joey added. "With the original Hawaiian stickers on it. Came out of an old house over at Rollover Pass. Husband passed away and the wife didn't want it taking up space in the garage anymore." A shake of his head and then more awestruck silence. "Can you imagine it?" he added in a whisper.

"Some people just don't know what they have." Logan edged forward to run his hand over the curve of the board and then stepped back. "Thanks for showing me," he said.

A moment passed, and somehow the two communicated without speaking. Joey nodded and then, with care, returned the board to the shed. Pippa waited until they were on their way back to Vine Beach before she asked Logan about the surfboard again.

"They just don't make longboards like they used to," he said as he signaled to turn onto the highway. "But I do."

"You do?" She shook her head. "You mean you make surfboards?"

The corner of his mouth turned up. "Does that surprise you?"

"It does, actually." Pippa brushed a strand of hair from her eyes and focused on the beach as it rolled past. "Something else surprises me, too."

"What's that?" he asked over the sound of the truck's engine and the rush of sea breeze from the open windows.

"Well," she said slowly. "You're dead set against getting on a skateboard and yet that Greg Nolt—"

"Noll," he corrected.

"All right. That Greg Noll surfboard looks an awful lot like an oversize skateboard without the wheels."

Logan glanced at her. "And yet they are nothing alike."

"You're a stubborn man, Logan Burkett. First you fail to see the brilliance of a pantry made from a British phone box and now you cannot admit there is anything similar between your hobby and mine."

He chuckled but said nothing further.

"What?" she demanded.

A shake of his head. "Just trying to imagine a girlie-girl like you on a skateboard." He shrugged. "No, can't see it."

So Logan saw her as a girlie-girl? Wouldn't he have been surprised if he'd spotted her on the ramp Saturday? "You *could* have seen it if you'd taken me up on my offer."

He slowed the truck to a stop at the red light and activated the blinker to turn onto Main Street. From the cab of the truck, she could see most of Vine Beach, including the Branson Building where she would soon live.

Those gorgeous green eyes met hers, a challenge in his expression. "So we're back to that, are we?"

Pippa lifted an eyebrow. "It appears so."

The light turned. A moment later, Logan pulled the truck to a stop in front of the Branson Building and then shifted the gear into Park and turned to face her.

"See you Wednesday," he said.

Pippa climbed out of the truck and closed the door. "Wednesday it is," she called over her shoulder as she headed toward the door.

"Oh, and, Pippa?"

She turned around. "Yes?"

"I'll let you know about the marble. It might require a trip to Galveston. Are you interested?"

"Absolutely," she said. "I've come to the recent conclusion that salvage yards are fascinating." But as Logan drove away, she decided that the handsome contractor was interesting, too. Extremely so, even if he was completely hardheaded and slightly frustrating.

Chapter Eight

Granny ran her finger along the edge of the antique partner's desk of their temporary downtown office and seemed to be looking out toward Main Street and the courthouse across the road. The look on her face told nothing of what she might be thinking.

It was Wednesday, two days after Pippa's foray into salvage yard oblivion down at Curt's. Though she had not yet heard back from Logan about his search for marble that matched what was already in the building, she assumed he was still looking. Pippa pulled out her iPad and quickly found the rooftop sketches Logan had sent over yesterday afternoon.

"Have you seen these?" she asked her grandmother as she turned the device in her direction.

"Enlighten me," her grandmother said with the slightest lift of her iron-gray eyebrow. "You know my old eyes don't like that little screen."

Old eyes, indeed. Granny's vision was every bit as sharp as her own. However, so was Granny's refusal to adapt to certain technology.

"It's absolutely breathtaking up on the roof, and Logan has this great idea to capture the space for a rooftop

deck. I hope you don't mind, but I told him to go for it."
Pippa paused. "As you can see, it will add quite a bit of
living space."

"I approve." Granny paused. "Although I still want to
see those blueprints."

"Logan said he would be bringing them."

Pippa rose as the bell on the ancient door rang, and
Logan Burkett stepped inside. He'd dressed the part of
a successful contractor for the meeting in khakis and a
button-down shirt a shade darker than his eyes.

Under one arm he carried a leather portfolio, and the
other hand held his aviator-style sunglasses. A pair of
boots in place of the expected business-type loafers was
the only hint of his blue-collar profession. On an ordinary
man, the outfit might have looked less than impressive.

He put away his sunglasses as he crossed the room in
a few long strides. "Good afternoon, Mrs. Gallagher."
He shook Granny's hand, then turned his attention to
Pippa. "Miss Gallagher," he said with the slightest hint
of amusement.

"Sit down, Logan," Granny said before Pippa could
respond. "We've been having the most interesting conversation about you."

Logan's eyes widened. "Oh?"

"About your idea for the rooftop living area," Pippa
hastened to say as she felt heat threaten her cheeks.

"I understand you provided my granddaughter with
a guided tour of this space." Granny's expression was
completely unreadable, something that rarely happened.
Usually Pippa knew exactly what her formidable grandmother was thinking, oftentimes before she showed any
indication.

"Yes, ma'am," he said slowly. "I did."

Granny lifted one eyebrow. "During my party."

Logan had the good sense to look ashamed. "Yes, and I apologize for taking her away from the event. I've got no good excuse, nor do I know what happened to my manners." He met Pippa's grandmother's direct gaze. "Will you forgive me?"

Granny's expression softened, though only for a brief moment. "Of course I will, Logan," she said, "though I do wonder what possessed you to take my granddaughter and just drive off. Pippa I can understand. That girl looks for an excuse to leave every time, but you, young man, well—"

"Granny, please," Pippa said. "Logan has apologized. Now, if there's nothing further, can we just talk about the renovation?"

A look of innocence crossed Granny's features. "I thought we were, darling. I merely wanted to point out that there is a time for attending to business, and you two chose…" She met Pippa's even stare and then brightened. "Well, never mind. I trust my point has been made. Now hand me that contraption you're holding, Pippa, and let me have a look at these drawings before we go any further."

Logan knew he'd probably catch some flack for leaving the party out the back door, but he hadn't expected it to come from Mrs. Gallagher. He'd stated the truth to Pippa's grandmother. He had no good excuse.

The rest of the truth would go unsaid. The part where he'd have to admit being intrigued by the girl he hadn't seen since high school. Where he'd say out loud that what little time he'd spent alone with Pippa Gallagher had provided some of the most interesting moments he'd spent in Vine Beach since he returned.

That he'd gone to sleep thinking about taking her surfing and awakened to continue the thoughts. Eric would say he had it bad for Pippa Gallagher.

And Eric would probably be right.

Thanks to his time at Starting Over, Logan thought he was prepared for risking his heart again. Whether that was true remained to be seen.

When he braved a look at Pippa's grandmother, he found her smiling. "So," she said in that regal way she had, "I've seen the small-screen version. Now let's do this the old-fashioned way and roll out the blueprints." When Logan complied, she nodded. "All right, now go on and give us your best presentation of what you'd like to do to return our lovely building to its former glory."

He began his well-rehearsed speech, using the blueprints to illustrate the plans he had for the three stories that would be renovated. Throughout it all, the elder Gallagher stopped him on occasion to ask questions but Pippa remained silent. Finally he wrapped up his presentation, then sat back and waited for the response.

"It's all very well thought out," Mrs. Gallagher said. "And I do heartily approve of what you have on paper. It matches nicely with our expectations and will still make the preservationists happy, yes?"

"Yes, ma'am," Logan said as he began to roll up the blueprints.

Mrs. Gallagher flipped the iPad around to look at the drawings once more and then shook her head. "Unlike my granddaughter, however, I haven't been treated to the grand tour."

"I can fix that." Logan grinned. "What if I were to offer such a tour, Mrs. Gallagher? Just the two of us?" He looked in Pippa's direction for confirmation that she understood he was intent on mending fences, not on excluding her. "Or you could join us."

"Yes, Pippa. I would like that very much." Granny gestured to her watch. "But before we do that, can you give me just a minute?"

"Why don't I go on over and unlock the building?" Logan offered.

"Yes, thank you," she said.

When Pippa made no move to go with him, Logan headed out the door and down the street to open the door of the old bakery with the key he'd been given. Before he could step inside, his phone rang. *Dad.* He sighed as he answered.

"Hey, sorry I haven't called you back, Dad," he said. "I've just been really busy and actually right now's not a good time, either."

"Just relaying a message," his father said. "I've got a potential buyer on the property. I'm taking him out to look at it the first part of next week. Do you think you can manage to get the neighborhood cleanup going before then?"

Apparently someone had the foresight to look past the questionable neighbors and see the property's potential. "That's great news," Logan said as his hopes soared. "We hadn't planned to do the cleanup so soon, but maybe we can move up the schedule."

"If you can, that's great. If not, I'll just explain to the buyer that it's in the works."

As soon as he finished with the Gallagher ladies, he'd be sure and call the Starting Over guys to let them know their prayers were being heard and possibly answered. He needed to talk to them about the neighborhood cleanup anyway.

"Sorry, Dad, but right now I'm with the Gallaghers over at the Branson Building. Can I call you later?"

"Give them my best."

"I will."

"And tell Pippa we missed her at family game night."
Logan laughed. "Goodbye, Dad."

Granny stepped back into the room with a smile.
"Ready?"

As Pippa grabbed her purse and prepared to follow
her grandmother inside, her cell phone buzzed with a text
from Rico Galvan. Broken window. Glass everywhere.
Doesn't look like anyone got in. Should I call the cops?

Pippa quickly responded. On my way. I'll call them.

"Something wrong?" her grandmother asked.

"I need to go check on something at R10:14." Pippa
pocketed her phone. "Rico said there's a broken window."

Concern etched the old woman's features. "Yes, of
course. Go."

Pippa retraced her steps to gather up her purse and
keys. Logan was waiting for her when she stepped outside. "I'm sorry, but I'm going to have to let you two take
the grand tour alone."

"Something wrong?" Logan asked.

For a moment, Pippa considered telling him about the
text. "Just something I need to check on," she decided
to say instead.

Granny reached to touch her sleeve. "You'll let me
know once you're sure everything is fine, won't you?"

After saying goodbye, Pippa slipped into her car and
made the call that would summon an officer to docu-
ment the damage. Then she headed to the warehouse
district, where she found a tight knot of skaters clustered around the side of the building where a window
had obviously been shattered. As she approached, several looked her way.

"We figured you'd want us to wait to clean up the mess until the cops came," one of the Crossley twins called.

Identical in every way but one, the fair-haired boys looked exactly the same unless they were aboard their favorite "rides." While Sean was a skateboarder, Seth preferred to do his skating in Rollerblades.

Surveying the damage as she made her way across the parking lot, Pippa was relieved to see that it appeared broken glass was the only problem on the exterior.

"An officer should be here soon," she told them. "Did any of you see what happened?"

The teenagers responded with similar negative responses. A moment later, a Vine Beach police officer arrived.

"Would you like to come inside?" she asked as he approached.

"No need," he said as he surveyed the situation and took a few photographs before turning around to motion for Pippa to approach. "Any idea who did this?" He looked beyond her to where the teenagers waited.

"No, they found this when they showed up for after-school skating."

"I see." He pulled out his notepad and jotted something down. "Can you tell me their names?"

Pippa did as the officer asked and then added, "I told them to leave it alone until you arrived."

The officer nodded and continued to write. "Anything taken or any doors opened?"

"Why don't we go inside and check?"

A few minutes later after determining no one had been inside the warehouse, he put away his notepad and pen. "All right. I think I've got everything I need. I'll be in touch if we get any leads."

"But you haven't taken statements from the boys."

"No need," he said, "unless any of you saw who did it."

"I didn't," she admitted. "And neither did they."

He shrugged. "Then I'll be in touch. Call us if you have any more trouble or figure out who did this."

"But that's your job," Pippa said.

"It is," he agreed. "But we depend on the assistance of the public. If anyone remembers seeing anything, let me know."

"Yes, I will." Pippa watched the officer leave and then turned to call the boys. "All right, I guess it's time to clean up."

"Don't worry," one of the twins said. "We'll take care of this."

"Thank you," Pippa answered as she hurried to unlock the door and step inside.

Instantly the heat hit her. Though it was a balmy eighty-plus outside, the interior of R10:14 felt like an oven. And it wasn't even the height of the coastal Texas summer yet.

During ministry hours, the garage-style doors were left open to the breezes coming off the Gulf of Mexico a few blocks away. Profits from last Saturday's event would provide an industrial fan to help once the July heat blazed.

Pippa crossed the space to open the door to the combination office and skate shop. An ancient sputtering window-unit air conditioner made the temperature slightly cooler in here, but the broken glass on the lone window was allowing most of the cool air to escape. Thankfully the burglar bars would not have allowed much else to leave the room.

Shards of broken glass littered the bare concrete floor and dusted the corner of her desk. Pippa picked up her copy of *The Brothers Karamazov* and shook it to send the splinters of glass to the floor.

"Got some boxes and tape?" the Crossley twin called. "I think we can fix up the window with that."

"Good idea," she said as she went to the storage closet for a broom and dustpan, then handed them over. "And what do you say I open the park early today? Call it a thank-you for all your help."

"Sweet." A grin, then he dipped his head. "But you don't have to thank us. We love this place. Kind of like a second home."

Pippa's heart soared. Of all the kids who'd crossed the doorstep of R10:14, Seth and Sean Crossley were among the toughest cases. Four months later, the pair had become the kid brothers she never had and the protectors she hadn't asked for.

She reached over to ruffle the skater's spiked hair. "You'll never know how much that means to me, Sean."

He looked up, surprise etching his features. "How'd you know it was me and not my brother?"

How *had* she known? Pippa let out a long breath. *Thank You, Lord.*

"I just did," she said.

A half hour later, the task had been accomplished and the half dozen teens were happily skating on the ramps outside her office door. When the phone rang, she rose to shut the door and, with it, most but not all of the noise.

A glance at the caller ID and she reached to answer. "Logan?"

"Hey, there," he said in his easy drawl. "Just checking to be sure you're okay."

"I'm fine," she replied as she returned to her makeshift desk in the back of the office.

One of the kids let out a loud whoop that carried

through the thin walls. "Pippa, are you sure everything is all right?"

"Yes, it's fine," she said quickly.

"Skaters?" he said.

"Yes. So, I assume the walk-through went well. Guessing you didn't get Granny on the roof, though."

"You'd guess wrong," Logan said. "I couldn't believe it but she climbed right up and had a look around. Apparently height is not something she fears.

"So," Logan continued, his voice cutting through her thoughts, "I was wondering if you had dinner plans."

"Dinner plans?" she echoed as the idea that Logan Burkett might be asking her out for something other than surfing took root. So did the idea that someone was knocking on her office door.

A second later, the door opened, and the same police officer who had taken her statement earlier stepped into the room. "Hold on just a second," Pippa told Logan as she regarded the officer with a smile. "That was fast. Did you get a lead?"

"No, actually when I got back to the station, this was waiting to be delivered. Figured I'd come back here and take care of it myself."

In his hand, he carried a sealed envelope. Her heart sank when he slid it onto her desk, then stood back to wait for her to open it.

Pippa knew what that meant. Someone had lodged another complaint against R10:14, and this time he had gone to the trouble to do it formally. What was it this time? The noise? Absurd because she made sure the kids stayed inside. Graffiti?

Ridiculous because the only tagging that had been done as far as she knew was on the R10:14 warehouse, and that had been at her request. So what if the Bible verses and names of biblical characters the kids had chosen were painted in a script that looked unreadable to some and suspicious to the rest?

Cradling the phone with her shoulder, Pippa broke the seal on the envelope and pulled out a stack of official-looking papers, the first of which was a notice and summons. The second page gave the list of complaints. Noise and vandalism were the accusations that had never stuck and yet here they were again.

What next?

The police officer cleared his throat as she met his steady gaze. "I'll need you to sign here, showing you've received this, Miss Gallagher."

Pippa drew in a deep breath and held up one finger to let the officer know she'd be with him momentarily. "Now, what were you saying, Logan?"

"Dinner," Logan said. "That's the meal traditionally eaten in the evening."

"Miss Gallagher?" The officer's tone was insistent. "You'll need to sign, please."

"Yes, I'm sorry," she told him as she opened the desk drawer to hunt for a pen.

"Pippa?"

"Logan," she said as she met the officer's steely stare, the pen now securely in her grasp. "Can I call you back? I'm kind of in the middle of something."

"Sure, but dinner? Let me know, all right?"

"I will." Pippa set the phone aside to sign the papers where the officer indicated and then handed them back to him.

"Court date's in the paperwork," he said. "Or you can appeal to the judge and pay a fine, but that'll depend on what he's willing to allow. Show up at the clerk's office during regular business hours and ask."

"I will," she said with the last of her strength.

"And, miss," the officer said as he paused in the doorway. "For the record, I will be looking into your vandalism incident."

Relief washed over her. "Thank you," she told him.

He dipped his head in a curt nod. "For all that's in those papers there, I have personally noticed that since your place opened, the kids I used to send packing aren't out there causing trouble. Those three you named earlier?"

"Yes?"

"They're good kids, and don't let anyone tell you otherwise."

Another smile. "I appreciate your saying that."

He shrugged. "Keep up the good work," he said as he made his exit.

"I will." After the door was shut and her privacy restored, Pippa let out a long breath.

The next day, Logan tried to ignore the fact that Pippa Gallagher had neither returned his call nor seemed the least bit interested in having dinner with him. It was short notice, he told himself. Next time he would plan ahead. Maybe make reservations in Galveston and take Pippa for a nice meal instead of an impromptu evening at Pop's Seafood Shack where her best friend, Leah, would be watching his every move from the kitchen.

Or maybe he'd forget about pushing Pippa into spending any more time with him than she had already committed to spend. After all, she did work with him almost daily on the renovations, even though technically most of their work involved emails and very few actual conversations.

Still, it was something.

And unless she changed her mind, Pippa would be surfing with him on Saturday morning. He thought of the Greg Noll longboard and her lack of reaction to the vintage treasure. Maybe once the property sold he would see what it would take for Joey to part with it and then he'd show Pippa what real surfing looked like.

As soon as he had the thought, he tossed it away. The money was not his to waste.

And neither was the remainder of a beautiful Thursday afternoon. After all, Logan had been at his desk working on the revisions to the deck plans all afternoon. Now they were done and so was he.

Logan rose to stretch out the kinks. He could drive to the job site and check things out. A grin. Or he could run there.

Ten minutes later, his running shoes were pounding the pavement on the way toward Main Street. A casual glance into the window of Gallagher and Company revealed neither Pippa nor her grandmother was at her desk, so he pressed on a few more steps to the Branson Building, where the door was locked tight.

Using his key, Logan let himself in. The remainder of the demo was complete and now the construction phase could begin. He rested his shoulder against the brick wall and surveyed the piles of construction materials stacked in the corner of the space that, beginning tomorrow, would become the interior of this building.

Six weeks of work, eight at most, and then he'd be free to go.

That meant he had six weeks, eight at most, to figure out where he was going.

Logan stepped back outside and locked the door, then headed down Main Street toward the beach. At the marina, he jogged to the docks in the hope of catching his stepbrother working on his sailboat. Like the Branson Building, the boat was locked up tight with no one around.

Turning back up the dock, he grinned as he spied Eric stepping out of his car. A wave and then his stepbrother headed toward him. "Good to see you," Eric said when they met halfway. "Looks like you're out running."

Logan nodded. "Care to come along?"

Eric met his steady gaze. "Sure, why not?"

A few minutes later, the pair were heading down the beach, the sun at their backs. Glancing over at Eric, Logan spied a smile.

"What's so funny?"

"Nothing at all," Eric said. "Just thinking of how long it's been since I took a run without pushing a stroller or measuring my pace to match a child on a bicycle. Not sure how to do this anymore."

Logan chuckled. "You're doing fine."

"But are you? Doing fine, I mean."

Logan gave Eric a sharp look. *Yeah* was the gruff answer he knew he wouldn't get away with. And yet he hoped he might.

"I appreciate your taking the boat out for me. She stays in port far too often nowadays."

"My pleasure," Logan said.

"I understand you convinced Pippa Gallagher to ride along." Eric made the statement so easily that Logan almost missed it. What he couldn't miss was his stepbrother's obvious curiosity.

"Yes, I did," he admitted. "And we had a picnic on Sand Island."

Eric nodded. "I used to take Amy and the girls there. We should do that again."

"Yeah, you should," Logan said.

"So," Eric continued, "are you and Pippa getting serious?"

Logan laughed. "Hardly."

And though Eric looked away, his expression told Logan that he was far from convinced.

They settled into an easy pace as they crossed the beach, dodging sun worshippers on towels and kids playing in the sand. Beach homes crowded the shoreline in tumbledown fashion, their pastel decks arching out over the sand.

Pippa lived in one of those homes, though Logan wasn't exactly sure which. Still, he couldn't help glancing over in that direction to see if he might catch a glimpse of her.

"It was good to see you on Sunday. The girls loved teaming up against their uncle Logan."

Logan thought of Eric's three daughters and their penchant for matchmaking that had culminated in Eric's marrying Amy. All three had taken advantage of Logan's rare presence at the weekly family game night to make their desire for a new aunt known.

Logan stepped around a sand castle someone had abandoned to the tide and then once again fell into stride beside Eric. "I know they mean well, but I'm fine."

"So you said."

Time for a change of topic. "Dad thinks I may have a buyer for Ashley's property."

Eric grinned. "Hey, that's great. Have you given any thought to what you'll do once that's handled?"

"Plenty." They rounded a curve in the shore and Logan spied the lighthouse ahead. "Race you," he said as he sprinted, leaving Eric behind.

Though the race was close, Logan reached the base of the old black iron lighthouse a split second before his stepbrother. Out of breath, he collapsed on the step and swiped at his forehead with the hem of his T-shirt. Eric settled beside him and then gave him a nudge.

"Clever, kid," he said. "But you didn't completely answer my question. What are you going to do once the property is sold?"

Logan rose and dusted off the sand. From this vantage point, he had a sweeping view of Vine Beach and the collection of buildings making up the city that was its namesake.

The longer he stayed, the less he remembered of his life in Zambia. Thatched huts and orphans with wide dark eyes were less distinct now when he recalled them.

No matter where he went, Texas would always be home. But the life he lived here seemed as far away as the life he had lived in Africa. And he didn't fit in either.

Eric stepped into his line of vision, his face wearing a look of concern. "Still don't want to answer the question?"

"It's not that. I don't know the answer right now," Logan admitted. "I just know I can't stay here."

"And why not?" Eric demanded as he stood. "What's wrong with settling in Vine Beach?"

"Too many memories," Logan said as he started back down toward the beach. "And not enough time to apologize for all of them."

"Then stop trying." Eric moved to stand between him and the path to the sand. "I'm serious, Logan. Just stop trying."

"That's easy for you to say," Logan snapped.

"Is this about missing Ashley or are you wallowing in guilt over what you've decided is your part in her death?"

"I'll never forget her," he said, "but I've accepted she's gone and moved on. What I haven't figured out how to get past is the fact that I put her on that plane. We fought, you know. She didn't want to go. I told her she had to. It's my fault, Eric, and that's something you cannot deny. You didn't make a decision that took your wife's life, so don't tell me how to handle it."

Anger flashed in Eric's eyes. Logan knew he'd gone too far, and yet he'd not apologize for speaking the truth.

"No, I just sat around and watched mine die of cancer and was helpless to do anything." Eric looked away, his expression tight. "Ashley got on the plane because you told her she should. Yeah, that's something you will always know to be true."

He paused to wipe his face. Logan remained silent, unwilling to argue and unable to change the subject.

"What you don't know," Eric said as he returned his attention to Logan, "is why. Or how, really. Or even whether it could have been prevented. You think you do, but you don't. And to take responsibility for not stopping something that God allowed seems to be awfully presumptuous, don't you think?"

Logan's jaw clenched and it was all he could do not to walk away. Or run. But would he be running from?

Or to?

That answer he did know.

"You've got to let this go," Eric said gently as he moved to clasp his arm around Logan's shoulder. "If you don't, the guilt will eat you up inside. You know what they say at Starting Over. Let God fix what you can't, brother. And stop beating yourself up."

By degrees, the pounding at his temples slowed. Finally Logan nodded. "Yeah, you're right."

"Yeah," Eric said. "I am."

Logan met Eric's stare. "I still don't know what I'm supposed to do after Ashley's property sells."

A shrug. "Doesn't matter. You'll figure it out."

"Yeah, I will, won't I?" Logan let out a long breath and then gestured to the beach. "Come on. Let's get out of here."

"Up for another race?" Eric challenged.

Logan lifted one eyebrow and then paused only a second before sprinting around Eric. Laughter trailed him even as his stepbrother gave chase.

This time as he passed the cluster of beach homes, he spied the unmistakable figure of Pippa Gallagher watching him from a deck beneath the shade of a large umbrella. The house was pale green. She was wearing a white, men's-style dress shirt as a cover-up for her swimsuit. She carried a book in one hand and a glass of what appeared to be iced tea in the other.

When he got close enough to see her smile, Logan slowed to a stop and waved. Pippa returned the gesture by lifting her tea glass.

"Can I interest you two in a couple of glasses of the house wine of the South?" she called as she leaned over the rail.

"Sounds good." Logan turned to Eric. "Don't you think so?"

"Wish I could stay but Amy's going to wonder where I am." He nudged Logan with his elbow. "And don't you forget you still owe me some work on the boat."

"What makes you think I won't have a glass of tea and then come help you?"

Eric shook his head. "You beat all, Logan. Really? You'd pick working on a boat over sitting up on that deck with Pippa Gallagher?"

Logan laughed. "When you put it that way…"

"Yeah, exactly." Eric waved up at Pippa and then returned his focus to Logan. He looked as if he wanted to say something. Instead he whispered to his brother, "Sure wish my daughters were here. I can't wait to tell them where I left Uncle Logan."

And then he was off, laughing as he ran. "Eric!" Logan called. "Don't you dare!"

But he would, and Logan knew it. A glance up at the deck, and he wasn't so sure he would mind just a little matchmaking. Or three matchmakers, that is.

And as he took the stairs two at a time, he knew for sure that if asked, he could tell his dad with complete certainty that at this moment he was running to and not from.

Chapter Nine

Pippa settled back into the beach chair and propped her bare feet up on the rail. Her legs were long and tan, her toes painted a vivid pink. A drop of condensation traced a path along the side of the tea glass and dripped on the hem of her shirt. She swiped at it absently, her attention focused somewhere out on the waves.

Rather than stare, Logan looked beyond her to the novel she'd set on the table beside her. A typical beach read had been his guess until he spied the title. *The Brothers Karamazov.*

She followed his gaze to the book. "I'm reading the classics this year. It's a personal challenge."

Logan said, "I see. Do you take these personal challenges often?"

Her smile was quick, radiant. "No, this is the first." And then the smile disappeared, a serious expression emerging. "I owe you an apology, Logan."

"And why is that?" he asked as he took a sip of tea and let the cold liquid slide down his parched throat.

The sound of a child's laughter distracted Logan. He glanced over to see a father tossing his son into the air, and his heart squeezed.

"I told you I would call you back and, well, I forgot." Pippa turned to face him. "I have a very good reason that I'd prefer not to discuss right now."

"As long as it wasn't another man." As soon as he said the words, Logan wanted to yank them back in. Thankfully Pippa took the statement as a joke.

"Oh, that's a good one," she said. "Although there was a time when I first got here that I did have random guys from church showing up at Gallagher and Company. Apparently a certain trio of matchmakers tried their best to fix me up."

"Might that be my nieces, the Wilson sisters?"

Pippa nodded. "The very ones. So watch yourself, Logan. The girls are persistent."

"So I've seen."

She lifted an eyebrow. "Oh? Have they taken you up as their latest cause?"

"I'm afraid so." Logan took another sip of tea. "At least that was the consensus at family game night last Sunday. So tell me, how did you get them to stop?"

Pippa shrugged. "I'm not so sure they have. It's possible they've just temporarily run out of eligible candidates. Vine Beach is a pretty small town, you know."

"Don't I know it?" he said under his breath. "So, tell me about Dostoyevsky. How's the book coming along?"

Pippa grinned and lifted the book to show him where a pink ribbon had been placed. "So far so good. The title page was extremely interesting."

"You've just started it, then." Logan watched her return the book to the table, happy to have a safe topic that didn't involve romance or matchmaking. "What was the last book you read?"

"Actually it was a screenplay, not a book." She met his gaze with a twinkle in her eye. *"Fiddler on the Roof."*

"The story of a matchmaker." Logan groaned. "Don't you love coincidences?"

"Oh, I don't know." Pippa sobered. "I'm not really given to believing in coincidences."

"No?"

"No." Another taste of iced tea and she set the glass aside. "We like to think of certain things as coincidences because it makes more sense to us. But what I cannot reconcile is how we can profess that God is in control and then claim that some things are mere chance." Her gaze collided with his. "What do you think, Logan?"

I think you have the most beautiful eyes.

He cleared his throat and tried his best to give the appearance of deep thought. "You make a good point."

"Of course I do." Pippa took another sip of tea. "So, is it true we're ready to start on the construction phase tomorrow?"

"Looks that way," Logan said. "I checked things a little while ago and all the materials are there and waiting. Just have to get the subcontractors to show up on time." He paused to shift positions. "The crew I chose comes highly recommended, so I don't expect any problems."

Pippa asked a few more questions about the schedule, and he answered them as best he could. Finally she nodded. "I'm very glad you're in charge and not me. I get to do the fun part."

"Which is?"

"Oh, you know. The decorating stuff."

"Speaking of which, I've finally got a lead on marble tiles that might work for your loft. I'm having the floor guy bring a sample with him when he comes to work on the hardwoods."

"Oh, good," Pippa said. "I really do like that part of the process, too. I didn't realize I would."

"You've got a good eye for design. Most people wouldn't think twice about tossing out the old cabinetry. I'm glad you could see the value in keeping it."

"Thank you." She paused. "And speaking of seeing the value in things, I still say that red British phone box would make an excellent pantry."

"Pippa," Logan said with extreme patience, "how exactly do you expect to get that phone box up those stairs and into your kitchen?" When she had no immediate response, he continued. "Exactly. You can't. It won't fit."

"And it won't come apart?" she asked timidly. "I did that once when I lived in an apartment with narrow stairways. We had to take some of the things up in pieces, but it all worked out."

"Sorry," Logan said. "Those phone boxes are welded together and are meant to stay in one piece. There's no way to take a metal phone box apart without ruining it."

Her frown was adorable. Logan could see the obstinate female had not yet given up the idea of owning that phone box. Unfortunately, unless she wanted to use it downstairs in the gallery, something he doubted the elder Gallagher would allow, given the traditional theme of the design features she had chosen, there was no place to put it.

"What about the extra French door?" Pippa asked. "Any thoughts on what we can do?"

"Several," Logan answered. "But it depends on what kind of décor you're going to want. If you're looking for more of a minimalist look, then there might be a problem fitting it in somewhere in the loft. But if you like the idea of playing up the age of the building and the patina of salvaged items, then I do have a couple of ideas."

"Logan," she said slowly as she leaned toward him, "are you sure you don't have any architectural training?"

An even look was all he spared her before shaking his head. "Stop changing the subject."

"That was a relevant observation considering…" Pippa paused. "You are impossible, Logan Burkett. But I forgive you, so to answer your question, I much prefer patina over modern."

"Then I'll do some measuring and see if my ideas are workable."

They sat in the dappled shade of the beach umbrella with only the sounds of the ocean and the rattle of ice cubes against tea glasses to interrupt the comfortable silence. When was the last time he'd just sat and enjoyed the warmth of the sun and the passing of time without looking at his watch?

Too long.

"So," Pippa finally said. "About dinner. Does your offer still stand?"

Logan met her innocent look. "Are you asking me to dinner, Pippa?"

"Of course not." She shrugged. "But if you were still interested in asking me, I'd probably say yes."

"Probably?" He pretended to consider this. "Then I probably ought to ask."

She lifted her tea glass to take a sip, then regarded him over the rim before placing it back on the table "Probably."

Logan let the silence fall between them again. Finally he pulled out his phone to check the time. "Pippa," he said when he returned the phone to his pocket. "I was thinking…"

"Were you?" Her response came out as a sultry set of syllables.

"Care to have dinner with me tonight?"

A chuckle punctuated Pippa's smile. "Funny you should ask. I was just thinking about that."

"Coincidence?" Logan asked.

"Absolutely not."

"Pippa, darlin', you're going to have to tell me which of my questions you just answered."

She rose abruptly and looked down at him. "Logan, darlin'," she echoed, "if you'll excuse me I need to get ready. You'll be back to get me in an hour, and that's barely going to give me enough time."

Just like that, Pippa Gallagher snatched up her book and tea glass and left him sitting on the deck as she entered the house. When the door closed behind her, Logan chuckled.

"How about that?" He finished off the iced tea in his glass and stood. "I have dinner plans and didn't need a single matchmaker to accomplish it."

Exactly fifty-five minutes later, Logan drove up and stopped a few yards away from Pippa's beach house. He'd put the top on the Jeep to be sure Pippa would be comfortable, air-conditioned and not windblown, and he'd even run the vehicle through the car wash and vacuumed most of the sand off the seats and carpet.

A quick look in the mirror and he froze. What was he doing? Acting like a teenager picking up his prom date, that's what. He sat back and let out a long breath. It was just dinner.

That decided, he shifted the Jeep into gear and pulled in. Before he could climb out, Pippa waved to him from the window over the driveway and motioned that she'd be right down.

Logan allowed a smile. Not a date. He wasn't ready for a date. But a meal with a client, now that was fine.

And then Pippa came around the corner and any notion of considering this a client meeting fled. She wore her blond hair in loose waves and a sundress and sandals in the same shade of pink as her toes. Logan cringed at the recollection.

Just dinner, he thought as he climbed out and hurried to open the passenger door for Pippa. *Just dinner,* he reminded himself as he tried not to notice that she smelled nice. Like soap and water mixed with something softly floral.

Logan climbed into the driver's seat prepared to ask where she'd like to dine. At this point he'd drive to Galveston if she asked. Or Houston. But taking her down the road to Pop's sounded good, too. Evening was beginning to fall and soon stars would be out.

Nothing beat sitting on the deck overlooking the Gulf of Mexico and digging into a meal of seafood that came off the boat that morning.

"How does Pop's sound?" Pippa asked before he could speak. "I just love sitting outside this time of day."

"Good choice," he said, trying not to mention the coincidence of his companion having practically spoken his thoughts aloud. Not that he believed in coincidence, of course.

A few minutes later, Logan was standing on the porch at Pop's Seafood doing the gentlemanly thing and pulling Pippa's chair out to help her into her seat. Overhead, crisscrossed strings of bulbs the size of giant Christmas lights flickered on, a nod to the coming twilight.

A waiter called Pippa by name as he delivered menus and water and then traded pleasantries. "One of my ministry kids," she said when the teenager was gone. "I'm grateful Leah gave him a chance. It's Ben's first job."

Logan was about to steer the conversation back to the skate park and mention the cleanup when Leah burst through the door and hurried toward them. "I thought I saw you here, Pippa, and…" She stalled a few steps from the table. "Logan?"

"Good to see you again, Leah." He picked up the menu and studied it even though he knew the thing by heart.

"And you, Logan." Leah pulled an envelope from her apron pocket and handed it to Pippa. "For the window."

"What?" Pippa shook her head. "I don't understand."

"Ben told us about the broken window. The kitchen staff took up a collection." She nudged the envelope into Pippa's hand. "Take it. You'll disappoint them if you don't."

Pippa accepted the envelope, then rose to hug Leah. When she returned to her seat, her eyes were misty. "Sorry." She wiped her eyes. "I just get so humbled sometimes at God's creativity."

"Okay, now," Leah said. "Put that away and let me feed the two of you. What're you having?"

Logan waited until their orders were taken and Leah had gone back inside before asking Pippa about the broken window. "I can fix those things, you know. I am in the construction business."

"I know," she said. "And thank you. Right now it's boarded up, so there's no hurry to make a repair. The kids certainly don't care."

"Ben must have," he said. "Kids don't just give away hard-earned money." He paused. "My misgivings about your methods aside, tell me what you're doing with this ministry."

Pippa leaned back and rested her palms in her lap, her gaze finally landing on him. "We've only been open a few months. Four, to be exact. I provide a safe place for kids to come after school." She gave him a warning look. "And really, that's what's needed with teenagers who have no real direction, don't you think?"

"I'm living proof of that." Logan hadn't expected to say those words aloud. But since he had, and they were alone on the patio, he continued. "I was one of those kids. Hardheaded doesn't begin to cover it. Dad did his best, but with Mom so sick…"

After a moment, Logan continued. "I took advantage and ran wild. Got in with the wrong crowd and eventually what happened to me wasn't in my father's hands anymore."

Pippa looked as if she wanted to ask but said nothing. He respected that about her.

"The year my mother died was the same year my dad sat in a courtroom and watched me sentenced to two years at the Giddings State School, which is a nice name for a not-so-nice place. On a dare, I had hot-wired a car and then crashed it. I wasn't even old enough to drive yet."

Logan pressed back the emotions and kept to the facts. "My sentence was commuted to time served, which was just under eleven months, but I think that was due in part to the fact I excelled on the football field." At her confused look, he continued. "What? You don't believe me? The Giddings Indians was the name. For obvious reasons we never played any home games."

He reached for the water glass and took a long drink, then set it aside to rest his hands on the table. Pippa reached over to put her hand on his.

"Anyway, I behaved and got to go home in time to use the football skills I'd learned in Giddings to play for Vine Beach High. Suffice it to say my senior year went a whole lot better than the previous year."

"Oh, Logan," she said in an almost whisper. "I had no idea. I'm so sorry."

He shrugged off the remainder of the memories and mustered a smile. "Hey, I turned out fine. Just had to do it the hard way."

Pippa removed her hand, and immediately Logan felt the absence. "So you understand."

"About what kids need to stay on the right path? Yes, I do. That's what I've been trying to tell you."

"Fair enough." She worried the edge of the tablecloth for a moment and then looked up at Logan. "What is it you think kids need? And don't say a new paint job on the outside of the warehouse."

"Discipline," he said. "Rules. Expectations." A shrug. "They need to know right and wrong and the consequences of bad choices. And they certainly don't need coddling. Didn't work for me."

"I see."

He looked at her. "Did I say something wrong?"

"No, no," Pippa answered quickly. "I agree with most of what you said. I'm just not sure how your ideas work in reality."

Logan flinched. "What do you mean?"

"I guess I come from more of a relational angle. I don't disagree that teenagers need to be accountable and there are definitely ramifications for their decisions. But I have found that offering a safe haven, for lack of a better term, has been very effective in turning kids around."

"Relational?"

"Sure," she said, her voice rising slightly. "Forming relationships with them. Earning their trust. That's how I'm reaching these teenagers. I was a skater kid, so I understand the ones who are different. They need a more gentle approach."

A more gentle approach? Again Logan thought of the skaters who were dragging down his property values. What they needed was a set of rules and someone to enforce them.

Pippa's expression darkened. His lifted brow must have given away more of his dislike of her method than he intended.

"You want to say more," she urged. "Go on and say it."

Seven years in the mission field in Africa had taught him a thing or two about booby traps. A man could be snared in what looked like an open field. The key was to know what to watch for.

Unfortunately Logan was in the trap before he knew to start looking. The question now was whether to keep talking or do damage control and change the subject.

"Here you go," Leah called from the door, answering the question for him. "Uh-oh. Trouble in paradise?" she asked as she set the tray on a nearby table and then placed their plates in front of them.

"Not at all," Logan said. "Just about to change the subject. Isn't that right, Pippa?"

She appeared reluctant to answer but finally managed a slow nod.

"I hope it's not a construction topic." Leah reached back to grab a bottle of ketchup and set it on the table and then stepped back to study the both of them. "Because if that's the case, then you've got to listen to the voice of experience."

"Good advice," Logan said.

"But it isn't. The topic, I mean," Pippa said.

"Oh?" Leah looked to Logan as if he might fill her in. Instead he reached for his napkin and placed it in his lap, then busied himself with adding salt to his potatoes. By the time he looked up, Leah had given up and was saying something about refilling water glasses. A moment later, she disappeared inside.

"That went well," Pippa said.

Logan met her even stare. "I thought we were going to try a new topic."

"Actually that's what you said. I haven't agreed to anything."

Chapter Ten

Logan set the saltshaker back in the center of the table and attempted a smile. "Not true at all," he said. "You agreed to come to dinner with me tonight, and for that I am grateful." He picked up his fork. "Do you have any idea how meager the contents of my pantry look in comparison to the bounty Leah has served here?"

Silence.

"Of course I have a regular pantry. Not one of those rusted red phone boxes that I hear are so amazing for storing my sandwich fixings in."

Pippa's expression was stony and yet, as she continued to stare, the beginnings of a grin appeared. By the time Leah returned with fresh glasses of water, both of them were laughing.

"Now, that's better," she said. "See if you two can keep things civil all the way through dessert. And by the way, the special is buttermilk pie tonight. Your favorite, Pippa."

"Let me see if I can manage all this first," Pippa called as Leah once again disappeared inside the restaurant.

The food was excellent, as always, but the company wasn't nearly as lively as when they first sat down. And the conversation was nonexistent. Not the comfortable silence they'd enjoyed on the deck. No, this was awkward with a dash of uncomfortable.

"Okay," Logan said as he set down his fork and faced her. "I owe you an apology."

Pippa said nothing, her expression hidden behind the water glass she held. When it appeared she would keep her silence, he continued.

"I'm an idiot. Please just know that I'm passionate about keeping kids from messing up like I did, and sometimes I don't exactly say or do things the right way." A pause while he sized up her reaction.

"Go on," she said slowly as she set the water glass back on the table.

"Go on?"

Pippa nodded. "Yes, you were defending the premise that you're an idiot. And I was enjoying it."

Her expression remained neutral. And then came the slight curve to her lip. The twinkle in her eye. And finally the giggle that let Logan begin breathing again.

"No," he said as he joined her in laughter. "I think I've covered the finer points. Glad to know I have been a source of enjoyment for you. Shall I continue?"

Pippa shook her head. "Logan, really, just eat, okay? And maybe when you get tired of being an idiot you could tell me what you were thinking of doing with that French door. And yes, I know you need to see if your ideas are workable, but I'd still like to hear some preliminary thoughts."

By the time Logan had finished his meal and the discussion on French doors and their multitude of uses, the sun had set completely, leaving the purple remainder of the orange sun. Pippa was smiling now, her mind back on that blasted red British phone box.

We'd like to send you two free books from the series you are enjoying now. Your two books have a combined cover price of over $10, but are yours to keep absolutely FREE! We'll even send you two wonderful surprise gifts. You can't lose!

Each of your FREE books is filled with joy, faith and traditional values as men and women open their hearts to each other and join together on a spiritual journey.

FREE BONUS GIFTS!

We'll send you two wonderful surprise gifts, worth about $10, **absolutely FREE**, just for giving our books a try! Don't miss out — MAIL THE REPLY CARD TODAY!

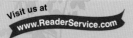

GET 2 FREE BOOKS!

HURRY!
Return this card today to get 2 FREE Books and 2 FREE Bonus Gifts!

YES! Please send me the **2 FREE books** and **2 FREE gifts** for which I qualify. I understand that I am under no obligation to purchase anything further, as explained on the back of this card.

**PLACE
FREE GIFTS
SEAL HERE**

❏ I prefer the regular-print edition
105/305 IDL GEJZ

❏ I prefer the larger-print edition
122/322 IDL GEJZ

FIRST NAME   LAST NAME

ADDRESS

APT.#   CITY

STATE/PROV.   ZIP/POSTAL CODE

"Pippa," he said in his best warning tone, "if you're not careful, you're going to show up at the job site one day and find out I have done something completely outlandish with your ridiculous phone box."

"I beg your pardon," she said with a decent mimicry of an English accent. "There are any number of uses for the phone box that are not the least bit outlandish if you would just stop thinking inside the box." A pause. "Box… phone box…get it?"

Logan groaned and tossed his napkin at her. Pippa ducked and came up laughing just in time to order buttermilk pie for both of them. By the time the meal was finished and they were walking back to the Jeep smiling, any evidence of their prior disagreement had vanished.

Twilight had given way to the thick darkness that fell hard on this nearly deserted end of the beach. Though there were beach homes close enough to reach on foot in a few minutes' time, any pretense of civilization here ended at the far edges of Pop's Seafood Shack's parking lot.

The sweep of the lighthouse's beam chased them to the car, illuminating the path as Logan closed the door behind Pippa and jogged around to slide into the driver's seat. Not since he stopped dating high school girls somewhere around the end of senior year did Logan recall feeling so nervous being alone in a vehicle with a female.

A female he'd gotten riled up before the salads arrived and then spent the last hour trying to make up to. For as much as it wasn't his fault, it was his opinions that sent the dinner conversation crashing southward.

Thank goodness for that ridiculous red phone box. If he hadn't thought to bring that atrocity up, Pippa would probably still be fuming.

"Thank you," Pippa said when he pulled the Jeep into her driveway.

Logan smiled. "Anytime. Now come on." He climbed out of the Jeep and followed her up the stairs to the entrance.

"You don't have to escort me, Logan." Pippa fumbled inside her purse, presumably for her keys. "This is Vine Beach, and I'm perfectly safe."

The keys tumbled from her fingers and fell between the steps to land on the driveway. "See?" he said as he bounded after them. "This is what I'm for. Fetching lost things. Now, which key is it?" When she pointed out the correct one, he opened the door and leaned in just enough to see that no one was hiding in wait. "Any bad guys in there?" he called.

"No bad guys." Pippa pressed past to step inside, her smile radiant in the moonlight streaming through the open door.

She shook her head and then reached for the light switch, illuminating a room decorated all in white. Not a single thing appeared out of place. Logan spied a novel on the kitchen counter, beside it what looked like some sort of journal. A blue pen lay atop the journal, the brightest spot of color in the room.

He glanced back at Pippa and found her watching him intently. Words eluded him for a moment. "No bad guys except me," he finally said.

"I think you're wrong," Pippa said.

"Again?"

"Yes. You're not a bad guy."

Her statement took him by surprise. "Please don't tell anyone. I would hate for my reputation to suffer."

A nod. "Your reputation is safe with me, Logan Burkett. Now, if you'll excuse me I've got an appointment with a couple of Russian brothers."

It took a second for him to figure out the reference.

"Ah yes, the Karamazovs. 'Love in action is a harsh and dreadful thing compared to love in dreams.'"

"Yes," she said softly as she pulled the keys from the lock and balanced them in her palm. "I actually just wrote that line in my journal this morning."

And there they were. The awkward moment where the moonlight slanted over her pretty features and his heart thudded to look at her. Logan took a step back. Lifted his hand in a wave. And then watched as she closed the door on a smile.

In all, not a bad evening. Not a date, but not a bad evening.

"I'm sorry, Miss Gallagher, but this time there's nothing I can do. Judge Cook says this is the second offense, so either you pay the fine or contest the matter in court." Becca Sue Sherman, the Vine Beach city court clerk, shrugged. "I wish I could help."

Pippa mustered a weak smile as she gathered up her papers and returned them to her purse. The fine alone would wipe out any profit the skating competition had made and completely remove the possibility of providing any more new Bibles or fans to cool the place for a very long while.

"Thank you."

"And, hon," Becca Sue said, "if I were you I'd keep those kids corralled indoors until this blows over. Unless you have a permit for an outdoor gathering, that is."

Pippa knew about those. The judge had denied the permit she'd requested for the skating competition, likely because of the complaints. Unfounded though they were.

"I wonder if it would be possible to make an appointment to speak to the judge."

Becca Sue winked. "I'll check." She came back a moment later and gestured for Pippa to follow her into the judge's chambers.

"Good to see you, Philippa." Judge Montgomery Welch gestured to the seat across from him. "What can I do for you?"

"I came to apply for another outdoor permit." She paused.

"I'll entertain the possibility," he said. "State your case."

"We followed all the rules you set for the indoor skating competition," she said. "The kids behaved themselves and kept the music down. I wonder if this proves to you that we're not attracting a bad element or causing trouble."

Those had been the judge's exact words when he had denied the permit before. Now he smiled at hearing them again. "Just one thing," he said as he picked up a file in front of him. "There's been a complaint."

"A complaint without merit," she said. "My kids aren't causing trouble. In fact, we're partnering with the Starting Over group at the church to do a neighborhood cleanup soon."

Judge Welch nodded. "Which creates a question, then. You're going to contest this?"

"It's a completely false accusation, so I would like to," she said, "but this is a small ministry that depends on donations, so I have to do what takes the least amount of money. According to Becca Sue, that would be to pay the fine. It's not fair, but I have to be a good steward of what God has provided to us."

Even as she said it, Pippa felt her blood pressure boil at the injustice of it all. She squared her shoulders and leveled an even look at Judge Welch. "Allowing us an outdoor permit will give us the ability to accept more skaters for our next event. And that will mean more funds to provide Bibles to the kids. And then there's the issue of industrial fans. It's already hot in there and it's not summer yet. I don't want to have to close during the months when the teenagers need us the most."

She waited only a second before continuing. "And it will give us a way to make up for the money we're losing in having to pay this fine."

"Yes," he said slowly. "I see your dilemma."

The gray-haired judge sat back in his chair and steepled his fingers. "You're a nice person," he said as he looked over the silver rims of his spectacles at her. "Raised well. Came from good people. Give me one reason why you're spending your time with these kids."

"They need me. And I've been told by someone in a position to know that I am making a difference. Even if I wasn't, I'd still keep trying."

The beginnings of a smile touched his face. "Yes, of course. And when would you want to hold this outdoor event?"

"Memorial Day weekend," Pippa said. "I should add that if we are allowed to gather outside, the plans are to have a Christian band play for the kids."

The judge nodded toward the door. "Pay your fine and then get the paperwork from Becca Sue, and I'll sign it. If you're willing to take these kids on and vouch for their behavior, then I'm willing to see they get some Bibles and an industrial fan or two."

"Oh, thank you, Judge Welch."

He waved away her response. "On a personal note, how much would it take to get these boys and girls some safety helmets? My wife, she's been harping on me to wear one when I'm cycling and the near miss I had a few days ago scared me into doing what she asked. I have to

think flying around on those ramps must require something like that, too."

"Well, yes," Pippa answered. "Yes, it does. We have
a few that they share, but—"

"But nothing," he said as he opened his desk drawer
and pulled out his checkbook. "And while I'm at it I will
throw in a fan." He looked up sharply. "This is between
you and me now," he said. "Just a grandpa wanting to
help."

Pippa thanked the judge profusely and then hurried to
complete the required paperwork. As she said her good-
byes to Becca Sue and headed back across the street, it
was all she could do not to let out a triumphant whoop.
What had been meant for evil...

When Pippa returned to Gallagher and Company,
Granny looked up from her computer to ask, "How did
it go? Were you able to get the complaint dismissed?"

"No." She told Granny what the clerk had said. "Paying the fine costs less than contesting the complaint.
However, I do have some good news."

Granny removed her reading glasses and shook her
head. "What do you mean? None of that sounds like
good news and yet you're smiling like the Cheshire Cat."

Pippa pulled the permit from her purse and set it on
Granny's desk. "We're hosting the Memorial Day event.
Indoors and out."

"But I thought Monty was refusing to give you a permit." She looked down at the page. "And yet here it is."

Pippa leaned her hip against the desk and grinned.
"He refused to give us a permit for the event last Saturday because of complaints. I've paid the fine, and he
sees no reason why we can't put on the Memorial Day
event indoors and out."

"That's wonderful, then."

"It is, but that's not all." She told her grandmother about the judge's donation.

"I love it when God is so creative. And the fact He used that stodgy Montgomery Welch to give those kids what they need." She shook her head. "You know he barely puts anything in the Prime Time Sunday school collection plate, so I'm thrilled he's finally let loose of his pennies."

Pippa laughed. "The amount was a whole lot more than pennies."

"Maybe I ought to go over to the courthouse right now and remind him he hasn't bought any tickets for the Ladies' Guild quilt raffle."

"You are incorrigible," Pippa said.

"Which is why you love me so."

"One of the many reasons."

Granny folded up the permit and handed it to Pippa. "Put that in a safe place. And go deposit that check before Monty changes his mind."

Pippa tucked the permit into her desk drawer and then snatched up her purse and left for the bank. The walk was short, just two blocks down Main Street, and the day was lovely. Her errand complete, she decided to walk past the Gallagher and Company office and go check on the progress at the Branson Building.

The doors and windows were thrown open to the April breeze, and inside a hive of workers swarmed around the various projects under construction on the ground floor. With so many people milling about, Pippa didn't dare go in and disrupt their progress.

She returned to the office to find Granny in the process of leaving. "Glad I didn't have to lock things up with you away," her grandmother said. "I wasn't sure you'd taken your keys."

Keys.

The word conjured up the memory of Logan racing to fetch her keys. Of his playing the gallant male and opening the door for her to be certain all was well.

"Pippa?"

"Oh, sorry." She walked to her desk and dropped her purse into the bottom drawer. When she looked up again, Granny was watching her with that scrutinizing look that generally preceded a grilling.

"Where were you just now?"

Pippa's attention snapped back to her grandmother. No way was she ready to talk to her about Logan Burkett. And if Granny pressed, what could Pippa say?

"Nowhere" seemed the safest response.

Granny continued to study her. "Well, then," she said with an appraising nod. "You should go back there more often. It suits you."

Notice of an incoming email chimed, giving Pippa the excuse she needed not to respond. The subject line was Construction Update.

"It's from Logan," she said just as Granny turned to leave.

Pippa glanced up at the clock. Of course. Friday at noon, regular as clockwork for the last month.

"Would you like to see the report?"

"I probably should take a peek." She came to stand behind Pippa.

Before Pippa could click on the report email, another appeared in her in-box. This one was also from Logan.

"Why don't you open that one first?" Granny asked. "There's no subject line so it could be anything. The other? Well, frankly, those construction details bore me to tears."

Pippa clicked on the second email, then waited while it opened.

Care to take a ride with me tomorrow to Galveston? Nine? The one in the morning.

"Well, now, I suppose one could make an argument for this being construction related," Granny said innocently.

Pippa looked up. "How so?"

"I don't know. I'm sure you'll think of something."

Chapter Eleven

True to his word, Logan arrived on her doorstep at exactly nine o'clock. He'd been ready since seven, but he'd never tell Pippa.

She wore pink again, a sweater in a pale version of the color she'd worn to Pop's, and a pair of white shorts that stopped just above the knee. Tiny pearls at her neck and ears matched the pearls on her sandals.

"What?" she asked when she caught him staring.

"You look beautiful." And she did. Truly without-a-doubt beautiful.

"But?" She glanced down at her outfit, then back at him. "Too fancy?"

"For Gaido's Restaurant? No. For Sal's Stone and Quarry, yes." Logan shrugged. "I probably should have mentioned that the marble my tile guy brought wasn't up to par. We're going to have to see if we can find something that works."

Pippa grinned, though inside her heart sank just a little. So it was construction related after all. At least she could truthfully report that fact back to Granny. "Okay. Give me just a second."

He watched her disappear into what he assumed was

the bathroom, then wandered over to settle on a bar stool in the kitchen. From his vantage point, Logan could see across the all-white studio-style space and out onto the deck and the Gulf of Mexico beyond. Nothing much indicated the personality of the woman who lived here, but then he assumed Pippa's things were in storage.

Or maybe she intended to buy all new once the loft was complete.

"I've got bottles of water in the fridge," she called from the other side of the thin wooden wall. "Help yourself, and would you mind grabbing one for me?"

He rose to do as she asked, and when he turned back around Pippa was standing there. In less than five minutes she had gone from glamor girl to fresh-faced beauty. Instead of the pink and pearls, she'd thrown on a pair of denim shorts and a T-shirt in vibrant turquoise with a college logo emblazoned on the front. A pair of running shoes replaced delicate sandals.

"Better?" she asked as she took the water bottle from him.

"Equally lovely," Logan said as he followed Pippa outside and waited while she latched the door.

The trip to Galveston took less than an hour, and while the conversation never lagged, Logan was careful to avoid the problematic topic of teenagers. Their first stop was the quarry where Pippa wasted no time in choosing exactly the right tile for the space.

The one he would have chosen had he gone without her.

Again, coincidence? Pippa would say no.

"That was easy," she said when they climbed back into the Jeep, the order placed and delivery scheduled. "What next?"

"There's a place over near Mechanic Street in the

Strand that I'd like you to see," he said as he backed out of the parking space in front of Sal's. "They do great work with iron, and I had this idea."

"Another one?" she teased. "Does it have anything to do with a phone box?"

"It does not," he said with mock irritation. "However, it does have everything to do with your new rooftop deck and, just maybe, the staircase to get up there."

Once they arrived at Vern's Ironworks, Pippa hung back to allow Logan to do all the talking. He noticed she was paying particular interest to a rustic chandelier and went over to stand beside her.

"That could work in the kitchen area of the loft," he said. "With the combination of rusted iron and cut crystal, it would look great, especially with the marble you chose."

She shot him a glance. "That's exactly what I was thinking."

"We think alike. That ought to frighten you." When she laughed, Logan linked arms with her and nodded toward the back of the shop. "Come on. I think Vern's got a sample of the staircase I want you to see."

The back exit led to a small courtyard not unlike the ones Logan seen in New Orleans. Instead of a bubbling fountain, however, a foundry and a metal table were set up with the accoutrements of the ironwork trade.

"Over here," the elderly Vern said. "I hired a new guy a couple of years ago. Gave him one job. Just make a staircase to the dimensions he was given. Nothing hard about that for a man with the experience he claimed."

When the guy paused to look back at Logan, he nodded. Vern went back to his complaining. "Turns out the fellow wasn't from around here. I mean I knew that the minute he opened his mouth, but I had no idea he assumed the numbers I gave him were metric."

He pulled a tarp away to reveal an ornate staircase in black iron exactly like the one Logan had in mind. The only trouble was the scale. This one looked as if it belonged in a child's world.

Pippa went to the piece and knelt to run her hand down the curved rail. "It's lovely," she said softly. "Like something a little girl would have in her playhouse."

"What do you think?"

She looked up at him, her smile broad. "Yes, I like it. Very much."

And I like you.

He liked her very much. Enough to consider her more than just a client. More than just a friend. How had that happened?

Logan looked away. "I'll go make the arrangements."

Pippa watched him walk away, his expression stony, and wondered what she'd done. She rose and dusted the rust off her hands but made no move to join him as he conversed with the craftsman.

Instead she took in the lean lines of a man who was not so far removed from his football playing years. Broad at the shoulders with arms that told of his strength at wielding a hammer, Logan Burkett stood straight and tall, his hands jammed into the front pockets of his cargo shorts, as he listened to the older man.

Her phone buzzed indicating a text. Rico.

Pippa quickly found the message and smiled.

Managing fine without you. Enjoy Galveston. I'll see that the park is locked up and all the kids have a ride before I leave.

She responded with a note of thanks and then looked back at Logan. He caught her staring and motioned for her to join them. She went reluctantly, unwilling to stop gazing at the man who had somehow slipped past the high walls she'd placed around her heart.

What she would do about that, Pippa had not yet decided. If only she didn't feel as though choosing to pursue some kind of deeper relationship with Logan meant she might have to give up the ministry she loved. It wasn't certain, of course, for they had barely spoken on the topic of ministering to troubled teenagers.

And yet his opinions on the topic differed wildly from hers.

Pippa reached the men and paused while the shop's owner described the process of making the staircase. He must have noticed her waiting, for he looked her way and grinned.

"I tend to like to hear myself talk," Vern said to her. "But that's because I don't have a pretty lady like you waiting on me. So let me fetch the order book and make this official so you two can get on with your day."

A short time later, they bade goodbye to Vern and walked down Mechanic Street toward the parking lot where Logan had left the Jeep. "I think you've made some good decisions," Logan said as they waited at the crosswalk. "Between the staircase, the marble and the chandelier, we've taken care of all the purchases that were needed today."

"Not completely."

He looked over at her. "No?"

"There's this place I like...." She shrugged. "Leah has taken me there a few times. You do know before she came back to run Pop's Seafood she was a restoration archaeologist, or some such thing."

"Restoration archaeologist?" Logan shook his head. "You made that up."

The light changed, indicating for them to cross the street. "I did not. Leah used to speak at conferences all over the world. Did you know she's working on plans to restore the main house at Berryhill to its original glory?"

Logan's interest piqued as he guided her across the parking lot toward the Jeep. "I remember that house. Never saw the inside of it, but I came up and rode the horses there a time or two. The house had been added onto over the years, but the part that was original, it was something to see. Legend is that house was built up higher than any place around, so the first Berry could convince his high-society gal that he was moving up in the world. Or something like that."

"Logan Burkett," Pippa said gently. "If you didn't profess to hate the architecture profession so much, I'd say you were talking just like one."

"I don't hate it." Logan opened the door for her and looked away preventing Pippa from seeing his expression. "I just don't intend to be part of it."

He closed the door, then stepped around to climb in beside her and started the engine. A push of a button allowed the salt air to drift through the interior as the electric windows slid down.

"Why not?"

Logan glanced over. "Why not what?"

"Why not become an architect? What's wrong with the profession?"

Logan shifted into Reverse and pulled out of the parking space. "Not a thing," he said. "There are plenty of good ones out there. However, I don't feel the need to join them. Now, where was this place you wanted to go?"

Pippa briefly considered challenging his stubbornness

on what was obviously an area of great talent. In the interest of keeping the peace, at least for now, she elected to let the topic go.

Yet another thing she couldn't speak to Logan about.

Shaking off the thought, she gave him directions to the two-story former hotel on Twenty-fifth Street where great bargains vied with great pieces of junk for attention. Five minutes into the shopping trip, Logan gave her a mournful look.

"You didn't tell me it wasn't air conditioned."

"You work construction, Logan," she said. "In Texas." Pippa reached beneath a giant rusted colander to retrieve a paper fan with the words Peaceful Valley Funeral Home on one side and a calendar for the year 1934 on the other. "Here."

He took the fan with a grin. "You do know how to make things tolerable, don't you?"

"It's a specialty of mine."

When Logan didn't laugh, Pippa turned away and kept shopping until he stepped in front of her. "You do," he said simply. "Make things tolerable, that is."

"Thank you." She intended the response to be flippant, a quick comeback meant to make him think his kindness hadn't touched her deeply. Instead her face flushed and her palms went clammy. What was it about this man that did these things to her?

Pippa snatched the fan from him and fanned herself. "You've got me all flushed now," she said in her best exaggerated Southern belle accent.

And then she spied it. The treasure that made all other treasures in this wonderful but haphazardly organized store pale in comparison.

The piece was covered in dust, but remainders of the rusty red color were unmistakably present beneath a layer of cobwebs. And while the piece appeared to be an original British Telecom box, the dimensions were only a percentage of what they should have been.

Too small for use as a kitchen pantry but perfect for getting up the narrow flight of stairs to the loft.

Logan must have seen it, too, for he turned to shake his head. "No, Pippa."

She grinned. "Yes, Logan."

"No, you can't." Once again, he moved in front of her, but she bypassed him and handed him the funeral home fan.

Sliding a cardboard box full of doorknobs and a set of stereo speakers out of the way, Pippa got the full view of her find. Indeed it was perfect. Dusty, yes, and in need of a little love and restoration, but it was exactly right for her loft.

Logan came to stand beside her and shook his head. "Really?"

She nudged him with her elbow. "Yes, really. Look at it, Logan. It's perfect."

"Pippa," he said with what sounded like the last of his patience, "you have no use for this. What in the world do you plan to do with it?"

"Something wonderful," she said. "Maybe turn it into a bookshelf or a fish tank or—"

"A fish tank?" He pulled a small tape measure out of his pocket and began to measure the height and diameter. "Do you have any idea how much this thing would weigh if you tried to fill it with water? It's just less than six feet tall and nearly two feet across. Once you start filling this thing up—if you could even get it to hold water—you're going to have an aquarium that will require the floor joists to be—"

"Spare me the construction lingo," she said. "You're good at what you do, and I trust you to make it work."

Logan jabbed at the top and then once again shook his head. "It's not metal, Pippa. And even I can't make a wooden aquarium hold water. Not going to happen."

"All right, so it can't be an aquarium. It's absolutely adorable and I want it. What we do with it will be something we can decide once we get it back to Vine Beach."

"Since this thing is British, I'm going to consider that you must be using the royal *we*. I know I never agreed to help you with it."

"But you will." Pippa offered a sweet smile. "Brace yourself, Logan," she said as she went off in search of the manager. "And make room in the Jeep. This treasure is going home with us today."

Ten minutes later, Pippa tried not to grin too much as Logan and the manager struggled to fit the phone box into the back of the Jeep. While the manager went off to look for more rope, Logan came to stand beside her.

"The only reason that thing is sitting in my Jeep is that it is made of wood. If it had been authentic and made of metal, there's no way we could have lifted it, even at the reduced size, and the shocks on the Jeep certainly wouldn't have allowed the weight."

"See?" Pippa said triumphantly. "It's almost as if it was meant to be. Here I've been wishing for a red British phone box and there it was sitting there waiting for me. And if you recall, I'm not the one who suggested we go to Galveston today." She bumped him with her elbow, then offered a dazzling smile. "Coincidence?"

"No comment," he mumbled as he spied the manager returning and went to help.

Once the treasure was secure, Logan started the Jeep and then pulled out his phone to check the time. "No wonder I was so hungry. It's almost two." He gave her a sideways look. "What would you say to a seafood platter out at Pier 19?"

"I would say that sounds heavenly."

He shifted the Jeep into gear and slowly pulled out onto Twenty-fifth Street, keeping a careful watch on the cargo in the backseat.

"It's very sweet of you to be worried that my phone box might fall out," Pippa said as she glanced back to see that the ropes and ties were keeping the piece securely in place.

"It's not that. I'm just worried it might land on someone and hurt them."

Pippa jabbed his arm. "That's not funny."

Logan pushed the button to turn on the radio, then slowed to turn left onto Broadway. "I love this street," Pippa said. "All these gorgeous old homes. Look, that one's been turned into a wedding facility." She squinted to try and read the sign. "'Weddings by…'"

Logan made a turn, leaving Pippa to wonder what the remainder of the sign said. She leaned back against the seat and looked up at the brilliant blue sky. With the sun on her face and the sea breeze drifting past, she closed her eyes and smiled.

"You look happy."

She opened her eyes to see Logan watching, the Jeep now stopped at a red light. "I am."

A nod and he went back to driving when the light turned green. Soon they arrived at the group of restaurants centered around the Harbor House Hotel. Logan paused to take a ticket from the parking machine and then drove into the lot to find a place near the waterfront.

Logan shut off the engine. then pocketed the keys and stepped out of the Jeep. "Coming?" he called.

She glanced back at the phone box. "What if someone tries to take it?"

"Pippa, my guess is there's not another person on Galveston Island who would want that thing." At her annoyed look, he gestured to the restaurant that jutted out over the water. "I'll ask for a table outside. That way you can watch over your treasure."

Chapter Twelve

Apparently Pippa got over her concern about losing the phone box to some idiotic thief, for by the time they finished lunch, she was ready to take another side trip. One that Logan was determined she would not influence him to take with her.

"Come on, Logan," the pretty blonde called over her shoulder as she stood on the wide concrete thoroughfare that snaked for miles along the eastern shore of Galveston Island.

Pippa had already persuaded him to drive over to Seawall Boulevard, a tourist-congested thoroughfare he'd been keen on avoiding. Before he realized what had happened, Pippa Gallagher had also convinced him to park the Jeep so she could take pictures.

"Seriously, Pippa. You live at the beach. What could you possibly find interesting about more sand and water?"

In response, she turned around to snap a photograph of him sitting behind the wheel, the ridiculous phone box still tied in place.

He put his hand up to shield his face. "Stop."

"Then get out of the car and come on." She lifted the

phone to take yet another photograph. "Too bad I can't get one with you smiling."

"Sitting here does not make me want to smile." Logan shook his head.

Pippa slipped the phone into her pocket. "All right, the camera is put away. Now will you come and ride with me?" She gestured to a spot on the other side of the road, and Logan turned in that direction. "Or maybe you'd rather go rent skateboards."

He spied the Rent Hut's sign apologizing for the lack of surfboards and frowned. So much for a decent counteroffer. Not that there was enough wave to catch this time of year anyway.

So she had him. He could either insist on leaving, which hadn't worked so well thus far, or comply and head across Seawall Boulevard to end up spending the remainder of the afternoon on a skateboard.

Or, more likely, falling off a skateboard.

Repeatedly.

With a sigh, he unbuckled his seat belt and pocketed his keys, then made his way around the Jeep to stand next to Pippa on the seawall. Even though he'd made regular trips to Galveston for building supplies in the past few months, he hadn't been out on the seawall in years. Not since he was a kid.

Strange that despite all the years and hurricanes that had come along in between, not much had changed. The Flagship Hotel might have been reduced to rubble and something resembling the Santa Monica Pier built in its place, but the seawall itself with the combination of tourists and locals was still just as it had been when he used to scare his mother by jumping from one granite slab to the other down by the water's edge.

"Which is it?" Pippa asked over the sound of the waves

crashing against those same slabs of granite some ten feet below the wall.

"Oh, come on," he said as he waited for the crosswalk light to indicate safe passage. Then he led the way across Seawall Boulevard to the palm-front-shaded entrance of Rent Hut. "Let's get this over with."

She caught up with him. "So we're skateboarding?"

"One of those ridiculous striped bicycle things, please," he said to the pimple-faced kid on the other side of the window.

"One surrey with the fringe on top," the kid called over his shoulder. Another kid in need of decent grooming appeared from the back room to offer a sleepy nod.

The price was highway robbery, but Logan paid it. Anything to get this part of the afternoon behind him.

The surrey with the fringe on top looked more like a lime green golf cart without the electric battery. Signs advertising various Galveston Island eateries and entertainment venues covered the sides of the vehicle while the back end boasted a sign in the shape of a football player that said Hut 1, Hut 2, Follow Me for Great Deals at the Rent Hut.

Covered with a canvas awning striped in the same neon green, the monstrosity was pedal powered with a steering wheel. Logan quickly climbed in and claimed the driver's seat.

In order to get the contraption to work properly, both he and Pippa had to pedal at the same time. Easy for him, but her legs weren't as long as his. Finally she got the hang of it, so they ventured out of the parking lot and, once the crosswalk indicated safe passage, across to the seawall.

With the pier and all its noise, nuisances and hub-bub looming on the left, Logan turned toward the right.

The late afternoon sun slanted across the road to collide with the stiff breeze rolling off the Gulf of Mexico. And though it was just the first week of May, the combination of warmth with wind felt just right.

So did having Pippa Gallagher on the seat next to him.

A click and Logan realized Pippa had taken yet another picture. "You're actually smiling."

Logan spared her a sideways glance and found the object of his thoughts matching his grin. Somehow while he wasn't looking, she had tucked her hair up in one of those messy ponytail bun things that was oddly attractive.

"Was not."

"Still are."

Of course he was.

They kept pedaling down the wide expanse of seawall, dodging the occasional tourist and even appearing in at least one family photo.

"That wasn't nice," Pippa said. "You totally photobombed that group of tourists."

"Photo-bombed?" Logan looked in the rearview mirror to see the dozen or so members of the Smith family staring back at them in their matching blue reunion T-shirts.

"Yes. It's when someone gets into a photograph by surprise. Usually it's not so obvious as what you just did." She turned back to face the front. "You drove right between them and their photographer just as he was shooting the picture."

"Unintentional, I assure you," he said. "How was I to know they were posing for a reunion photo?"

"Might have been the way they were all lined up with the taller ones in the back and the kids in the front." Pippa giggled. "Or maybe it was the guy with the camera on the tripod giving them all instructions on where to stand. Oh, then there was the big sign that the tall guy in the back was holding. It said 'Smith Family Reunion.'"

"I saw two sets of people with a plenty of space between them for this ridiculous cart to fit through. The only place to go was between the tripod and the tourists." Logan shrugged. "It's these kinds of decisions that make great leaders."

He attempted a serious expression but ended up laughing along with Pippa. The truth was he'd been too busy thinking about the woman sitting next to him to pay attention to anything else. Thinking about how he had never expected to spend a necessary day in Galveston with her and end up liking it so much.

Liking her so much.

They rode in silence awhile longer and then Pippa spied the ice cream vendor. Two chocolate cones later, they were happily on their way again. By the time the sun had slid behind the line of hotels on the other side of the seawall, Logan had almost forgotten how very much he hadn't wanted to go along with Pippa's plan to visit the seawall.

Then he got a glimpse of just how far away the Jeep was. Barely a speck on the horizon, it was visible only because of the ridiculous red British phone box lashed to the roll bar.

Logan paused to steel himself for the drive. He'd run marathons when he was younger, so this was nothing. Or so he told himself.

By the time they reached the Jeep, Logan's legs felt like jelly. He was about to say so when Pippa leaned over to press her cheek against his. "Smile!"

He heard the click before he realized she had taken a picture.

"Come on," she said. "Stop making faces."

Logan glanced at the photograph on the phone's screen. There was Pippa, looking like a vision, and right next to her was a guy who appeared to be in complete shock.

"One more time," she said as she pressed her cheek against his. This time when the camera snapped, Logan made sure he was looking at it and that his expression was something other than ghoulish.

"Thank you," she said as she slipped the phone back into her pocket. "It has been a perfect day."

She climbed out looking as fresh as when the ride began. He left her at the Jeep and maneuvered the surrey across four lanes of traffic to return it to the Rent Hut. By the time he made his way back and climbed behind the steering wheel, Logan knew he'd be applying extra-strength pain relief gel to both legs before he went to bed.

Pippa appeared to be suffering none of the leg aches he endured all the way back to Vine Beach. Instead she alternated between commenting on the sunset and leaning back against the seat to look up at the stars.

"Are you getting cold?" he asked when he spied her rubbing her arms.

"Maybe a little," she admitted, "but we're almost home now."

"Nonsense." He pulled the Jeep over on the side of the deserted highway and reached under the seat to pull out the sweatshirt he kept stowed there. "Put this on. It's clean, I promise."

The sweatshirt was soft and cozy and smelled faintly of laundry detergent. Pippa buckled her seat belt once more and then snuggled into the warmth as Logan steered the Jeep back onto the highway. Though Pippa knew Vine Beach was at least another fifteen minutes away, the lights of the city were on the horizon before she realized time had passed.

When Logan stopped the Jeep in the driveway, there was no question of whether he would walk Pippa to the door. It was dark. That's what he did.

The question was what they would do with Pippa's newly acquired treasure. She nodded to the phone box. "You can't get that out of there by yourself."

Logan groaned. "I can't very well leave it, and you certainly can't lift it."

Pippa leaned against the stair rail and, try as she might to stifle them, the giggles began. "I guess there's just one thing to do."

"What's that?" he asked as he stood behind the vehicle, hands on his hips.

"You're just going to have to leave it in the Jeep until someone can help you with it," she managed as she laughed. "I'm sure I can find someone." Another round of giggles. "Tomorrow."

"You're not serious. You expect me to drive to church like this?"

She attempted a somber expression as she shrugged. "The phone box made it all the way from Galveston. I think it will probably be safe to drive around town with."

Logan stepped into the circle of light from the streetlight. "You're enjoying this, aren't you?"

"Of course I am. Now come on up and let's see if there are any bad guys up here other than you."

Logan reluctantly followed her upstairs and then waited while she opened the door and turned on the lights. With nothing amiss inside, Pippa walked across the room to toss her purse on the kitchen counter. Her companion, however, remained at the door, apparently reluctant to come in.

"Can I offer you a glass of tea?"

Hesitating a second, he finally nodded. "Sure."

"Then close the door so the bugs don't get in."

He did as she asked and then settled at the counter while she pulled out two glasses and filled them with ice. While she retrieved the pitcher of tea and filled the glasses, she noticed Logan had found her copy of *The Brothers Karamazov*.

"Did you finish it?"

"I did," she said. "And right on time." When he looked confused, she explained. "I read one each month so I had to finish the April book before it became May this week."

"I see. So tell me." He set the book aside and accepted the glass of tea. "What made you resolve to read the classics this year? Just something you thought of?"

Pippa kicked off her shoes and grabbed her tea glass then nodded toward the deck. "It's nice out. How about we take our tea outside and I'll tell you all about it?"

Logan rose to follow her. The moon rode high in the distance, tracing a silver path across the waves and up the sand to stop at the deck. Pippa settled in the chair beside him and propped her feet on the rail, crossing her legs at the ankles. After letting out a contented sigh, she placed her tea glass on the table between them.

"It started last Christmas," she said. "I had just left the job in Dallas and closed up my apartment there. My things were actually on the truck and being delivered on December twenty-sixth."

"Not the best time to be moving," he said.

"Not at all, and yet in a strange way it was perfectly timed. The whole family had been together the week before. Aunts, cousins, even my mom and dad were here. They live in Sumatra most of the time. Mom and Dad, that is. They have since I was a little girl."

"I see."

"The afternoon of the twenty-fifth, everyone parted

ways. Granny, my aunt and the cousins flew to Dallas and my parents were due back at the mission house in Indonesia. By the time the sun set on Christmas, I had Granny's house to myself."

Logan remained quiet, and for that Pippa was glad. "What did you do alone in that big house?" he finally asked.

"What I had always done. I went into Granny's library and found a book." She shrugged. "Honestly I was looking for something that wouldn't require too much in the way of thought, you know?"

When he nodded, Pippa continued. "The house was new, and there was nothing but the classics in the library. Later I found out that Granny's decorator had banished all Granny's novels to boxes in the attic and bought the books by the pound. She organized them on the shelves by color so the room would look more elegant." Pippa took another sip of tea. "But I didn't know that then. I figured if Granny liked these, then I should, too. I closed my eyes and picked the first book my hands touched."

"What was it?"

"A Tale of Two Cities."

"'It was the best of times, it was the worst of times…'"

"Exactly." She returned the tea glass to the table. "Oh, how I loved that book. By the time the movers arrived the next morning, I was halfway through it. All I wanted to do was keep reading so I could find out what was going to happen to Sydney Carton, Charles Darnay and Lucie Manette."

"I still remember the ending."

She reached across to touch his elbow. "Oh, Logan, wasn't that just the best?"

"It was."

Pippa sighed and then shifted positions. "So, after I

finished unpacking, I decided I would do some research and find a list of classics to read. One each month for the whole year. *The Iliad* is the May book."

"What's coming up in June?"

"Why? Want to read along with me?" She giggled. "Maybe form a Classic of the Month book club?"

"Now you're just being silly. What's the title?"

"For Whom the Bell Tolls."

"Hemingway?" He shrugged. "I might be interested."

"Or you could wait until July. I'll be reading…" A flash of light in the eastern sky caught Pippa's attention. "Look. It's a shooting star. Oh, Logan, I haven't seen one of those in ages."

"Neither have I. Not since Zambia."

"Tell me about Zambia." The words tumbled out before she could stop them, an innocent request made in the comfort of twilight.

Logan's sigh was soft, barely audible over the lapping of the waves against the shore. "Zambia. Hmm." He paused and seemed unwilling to go on.

"Tell me about your wife," Pippa said gently, emboldened. "Or don't, if you don't want to."

At first she wasn't sure he heard. And then he cleared his throat. "Ashley. Her name was Ashley Trent. You might remember her from Vine Beach High."

She did, vaguely, but to say so might interrupt the moment. So Pippa kept quiet.

"We were kids, way too young to get married, but thinking we were way too old to be told what to do. We were going off to save the world. Funny thing is, I can't remember which of us thought that was a good idea. Seemed like one day I was a kid and the next I was a married man hauling all my worldly goods onto a propeller plane and unpacking them on the other side of the world."

"Are you sorry you did it?"

"Go to Zambia? No. Get married?" A pause. "Yeah. Sometimes."

Silence fell between them as Pippa left Logan to his thoughts. Ice in one of the tea glasses shifted, clinking against the surface.

"I was so mad at her," he finally said. "We fought. A lot. Stupid stuff, but then we were just kids. But the day I sent her home?" He shook his head. "We were done. A mutual decision. We figured it was a blessing there weren't any children involved. Just a clean break and maybe a fresh start elsewhere. For her anyway. I was going to stay right there." A glance at Pippa. "I've never told this to a soul."

"And you don't have to tell me. It's okay if you don't want to."

"No, I do." A deep breath and then he let it out slowly. "She had lied to me. I told her that was the one thing I wouldn't tolerate, but she did it anyway. And you know the funny thing?"

"What's that?"

"I can't even remember what she lied about." Logan sat very still and quiet. "But it was enough that I was finished and she agreed. I drove her to the little airstrip just in time for her to catch the weekly plane to the city. It was raining, nothing out of the ordinary for that time of year. She wanted to wait and go in a week or so when the next plane came through."

Logan rested his arm on the table. His fingers drummed the surface for a moment, and Pippa wasn't sure he would continue.

"I told her I couldn't look at her and know she'd lied to me." Logan captured Pippa's gaze. "I said those exact words. Then I drove off and left her there. The plane didn't get two kilometers away from the airstrip before it went down."

"Logan. I'm so sorry." Pippa reached over to place her hand on his arm. It was a pitiful gesture considering the depth of emotion he'd just shown.

"I stayed where I was until I couldn't stand living the lie anymore. I wasn't a grieving husband, I was a guilty widower. So I got on the internet and found a job in the farthest location I could get from Zambia. I called home and told Dad I was moving to Alaska to build houses. I had experience from trying to keep the hut we called an office and home from falling in, and no one in Alaska thought to question a guy with a missionary background about his qualifications."

"What brought you back here?"

"Dad. He didn't beg or preach. Last November he sent me a one-way open-ended ticket with a one-word note."

"What was that word?"

"Please."

The same word Granny had used to get her home. Pippa offered a knowing nod.

After a moment, she moved her hand away. Logan took the opportunity to finish off his iced tea and then stood. "I should get going."

Pippa rose to follow him back inside, taking his tea glass and depositing it in the sink along with hers. When she turned around, she caught him looking at her with the oddest expression.

"What?" she asked.

Logan seemed about to respond, then shook his head. "I guess I'm taking your phone box home with me tonight."

"I guess so," she said. "Unless you'll let me help you unload it."

"I will not."

Pippa shrugged. "Then let me come by and pick you up for church. I owe you that much."

"You don't owe me anything," Logan said. "But I admit I wasn't looking forward to explaining the ridiculous red box lashed to my car."

Pippa snagged a dish towel and reached to swat at him with it. She missed intentionally. "Go on home, then," she said. "Just be careful with my phone box and promise me you won't take a liking to it and forget to give it back."

"Oh, I promise. And unless I miss my guess, I can probably convince a couple of the guys from the Starting Over group to come by tomorrow afternoon and deposit it into your garage."

"Or maybe just take it over to the loft," she suggested. "Since that's where it will end up anyway."

"Good idea. And though I appreciate the offer, I won't need a ride. I can borrow Dad's Harley." He moved toward the door. "Tomorrow at the loft, then?"

They set a time and then Pippa stepped outside to watch him jog down the stairs. "Ouch," she heard him say when he reached the driveway below.

"Are you all right?" she called down into the darkness.

"I'm fine." He stepped into the glow of the streetlight and looked up at her. "But I think I used muscles today that I didn't know I had. That surrey ride turned out to be brutal."

She knew she'd be sore tomorrow, too, but the ride had been anything but brutal. From her recollection, every moment of it had been wonderful.

Even the part where they accidentally ruined the family reunion photograph. Now, that was a picture she'd pay good money to have.

Pippa stood at the door until the taillights of Logan's

Jeep disappeared down the road. Then she went inside and locked the door—and realized she still wore Logan's sweatshirt.

She turned out the lights and padded into the bathroom to slather cream onto her face, then brushed her teeth and changed into her pajamas. Just before climbing into bed, she reached for Logan's sweatshirt and put it on.

Drifting toward sleep, Pippa lifted the sleeve to her nose and smelled the soapy cleanness. What would she do about Logan Burkett?

Chapter Thirteen

At Judge Welch's request, the first skating competition had been a relatively under-the-radar event with most of the attendance because of the skaters' spreading the news among themselves. No banners, no splash of publicity. Just a bunch of kids having a good time on the sly, as Rico termed it.

The Memorial Day Skating Bash would be just the opposite.

As a former events planner, Pippa loved every minute of the preparation that went into this kind of thing. But as the owner of a skate park ministering to kids who needed her, she hated to think what could happen if anything went wrong.

The warehouse was quiet this Tuesday afternoon, the kids still not yet released from school for the day. So Pippa leafed through several pages of notes in the event binder she kept until she found the phone number she was looking for. A DJ on the Christian radio station in Houston had recommended an up-and-coming local band, and after listening to a few of its songs on iTunes, Pippa was convinced the kids would love it, too.

A few minutes later, she checked that item off her list,

the band more than happy to oblige at a greatly reduced rate. Next came the advertising. She had planned to make a big splash: put out radio ads and maybe even get Rico to draw up some sort of print ad that could run in a few local publications.

Pippa rose to stand at the newly repaired window and look out over the parking lot where in less than a month a bandstand would go up and a throng of skaters would spend the day having a great time.

It would be a huge day for the ministry. A ministry that the man she was coming to care deeply for didn't agree with.

Pippa pressed her palm to the windowpane. A storm was brewing over the Gulf of Mexico, one of those late spring showers that cropped up. The wall of gray and the chill wind that swirled around it echoed her mood. She turned back and busied herself whittling down her to-do list until the skies opened up and the rain began to fall.

A rumble of thunder told her the storm might be more than a passing shower. With weather like this, the likelihood of kids coming to skate was low. She texted Rico to let him know she was closing the warehouse for today and then put up a sign on the door for any of the more daring teenagers who might show.

Finally she ducked through the rain to climb into her car, grumbling at the design feature on her car that allowed a stream of water to pour onto her leg at a steady pace until the door was shut tight. She reached into the miniscule backseat to fetch the beach towel she kept for such emergencies, only to find Logan's sweatshirt in her hand.

Once again Pippa held the sleeve to her nose, rainwater still dripping down her leg. Placing the sweatshirt on the seat beside her, she felt around in the back until she found the towel wedged between the seat and the floor. Mopping at her leg, she sat back to consider her options.

With Granny expecting her to be busy at the skate park, her presence would not be required in the Gallagher and Company office, so going home was the obvious choice. Or, she thought as she glanced over at the sweatshirt, she could go and find Logan.

Folding the towel, she swiveled to tuck it back into place behind the seat. Her fingers touched something, a book, and she pulled it out into view.

A copy of Rico's New Testament.

Yes.

She placed it on top of the sweatshirt and started the engine. It was time to see a contractor about a situation in need of repair.

Pippa found Logan perched on a ladder, screwing the last of the lightbulbs into the iron chandelier she'd purchased in Galveston. She watched him complete his work in silence, not wanting to surprise him and make him fall.

When he stepped down to reach for the light switch, she cleared her throat. His gaze met hers just as the lamp blazed to life overhead.

"Oh, Logan, it's beautiful." Pippa glanced around to see what appeared to be the new spiral staircase sitting in the alcove. "And he brought the stairs, too?"

"Hello, Pippa." He grinned. "To answer your question, he brought stairs, yes, but not exactly the ones we ordered."

"I don't understand." She moved toward the alcove. "This looks very similar."

"It is. Vern sent word that since his crew was coming today to bring the chandelier, he would add in this piece on spec. If we like it, we keep it. If not, then we let him know and he sends his guys to come get it and replace it with the one you ordered." Logan came to stand beside her. "The dimensions are the same, but if you look at the details of the stair rail and iron spindles, they aren't an exact match."

Pippa looked closely and found that while the original design was more embellished, this staircase had a more clean-lined look. "You know," she said as she inched toward the wall to view it from a different perspective, "I think I like this one better. It just seems to fit. Like it has always been here."

"That's what I thought, but the final decision has to be yours."

"Then I say it stays."

Logan glanced down as she pulled his sweatshirt from her bag. "What's that?"

"Thank you for the loan." Pippa handed him the shirt and then set her bag aside. "It's clean. I promise."

Their eyes met again and slowly Logan grinned. "I had a great time on Saturday." He looked at the sweatshirt and seemed to be recalling the day. "Sunday not so much."

Pippa laughed at the thought of Logan and two of his friends from Starting Over struggling to extricate the phone box from its place in the backseat of the Jeep. Compared to untying the knots and cutting through the restraints that held her treasure in place, hauling the thing up the stairs and into the loft had been easy.

Well, relatively so.

Likely Logan would feel the bruise where the edge of the box jabbed him in the ribs for quite a while.

"What are you going to do with that thing?" Logan gestured to the phone box. "And no, I haven't changed my mind about allowing you to turn it into an aquarium."

"Nothing of the sort." Pippa paused to offer a smile.

"I've got an idea, but I'm looking for a good carpenter to help me with it. Know where I can find one?"

Logan feigned innocence. "No," he said slowly, "but I know where you can find an excellent carpenter. Now tell me what you have in mind."

"I was thinking the box would make a great computer workstation. With a shelf at table height to hold the computer and maybe another just beneath for the keyboard? Oh, and you would probably have better ideas on it than me, but I figured maybe there would be a way to hide a printer in there somewhere. You know, out of sight and yet accessible. I hate seeing wires running all over the place, and I'm not keen on having my computer just sitting out, either. So the door would need to remain functional—then I could close it when I don't want to look at the electrical stuff."

He gave her an appraising look. "I like it."

"You do?"

"Yes, I do. And I'm sure I can come up with something to make that thing useful." At her scolding look, Logan amended his comment. "That is, I'm sure I can adapt your interesting find to your specifications." Folding the sweatshirt, he deposited it on the ladder. "In the meantime, come see the progress on the rest of the building."

The tour began downstairs and continued back in the loft, where he pointed out the newly renovated bath just waiting for the marble she picked out on Saturday.

Pippa spied the French door from the salvage yard and smiled. "The door is perfect here. I love that you were able to preserve the patina and still make it sturdy enough."

Logan shrugged. "Long as you don't mind having windows in your bathroom door, who am I to judge?"

She laughed. "I told you I was going to put up sheers.

Or maybe spray some of that stuff that makes the windows look opaque."

"I can do that for you," he said. "Make the glass opaque, that is. Curtains? You're on your own there." Logan paused. "Actually I had an idea for the other door. Come and see what you think."

Pippa followed him to the corner where the kitchen was quickly taking shape and watched while he drew a rough diagram of the loft. As he leaned over his work, she recalled the photograph of him she'd taken with her phone. He'd worn the same look of concentration then, had been completely unaware of her attention.

Just as he was now.

He glanced up. "Something wrong?"

Yes. "No."

A curt nod. "Well, here's my thinking." Logan showed her how choosing a smaller staircase had freed up just enough space to put in the pantry the kitchen lacked. The one she'd hoped to gain with the original British phone box.

Pippa leaned in to see the broad strokes of his pencil as he sketched the changes he had in mind. Only when his hand paused did Pippa give the slightest thought to the fact that he stood very close. Lightning crackled outside, and she jumped.

Logan reached to steady her, and his arms lingered on hers. His eyes met hers. The rain pelted the windows and filled the silence that sizzled between them.

Slowly his hands slid down her arms to grasp her fingers and entwine them with his. Slower still, he brought her fingers to his mouth, his eyes never leaving hers.

This was not why she came to the loft today. Not why she wanted to see him.

But, oh. Oh. This was... Even her thoughts became

a jumbled mess as Logan pressed his lips to her knuckles. Still their connection, the gaze that held her in place, did not waver.

"Pippa." His voice was soft. Gentle. Slightly ragged at the edges. "Pippa, I…" He shook his head, his lips once again grazing her hand. "That is, I want to kiss you."

She leaned in, just slightly. "Yes." The word fell into the space between them as she closed her eyes.

"Yes?" he asked softly, Logan's breath now warm against her cheek.

"Logan?" someone called from downstairs, and the enchantment was broken. "Logan, are you up there?"

He released his grip and took a step back as the sound of heavy footsteps stomped up the stairs toward them. "Dad," Logan said when his father appeared.

Riley Burkett greeted Logan and then turned his attention to Pippa. "I'm sorry. Am I interrupting a business meeting here?"

"No," she managed to say. "We were just…" Pippa looked to Logan to help with the words that had gone missing along with the more addled parts of her brain.

"I was showing Pippa the plan for the French door that matches the one on the bathroom. I would like her to consider putting it on the new pantry."

A nod. Yes, she could handle that. But standing on legs that had endured the long ride in the Galveston Island surrey without much of a twinge? That was quickly proving impossible.

Riley now wore a half grin that warned he suspected something might be up beyond construction plans. Or at least that's how it seemed to Pippa. "Well, I can come back later."

"No," they both answered. This time a look passed between them.

It appeared the elder Burkett's suspicions rose with his iron-gray eyebrows. "All right, then." He turned his attention to Logan. "If I'm not interrupting, then, son, could I speak to you about something? I've got some news, and you've got a decision to make. A quick decision, actually."

"I'm just going to leave you two alone," Pippa said as she snagged her bag and hurried toward the stairs.

"The pantry," Logan called. "Is that a yes? I can start framing it out today."

A nod and a wave and she hurried down the stairs and out the door, not slowing until she reached the safety of her car. Inside, with the rain still streaming down on her leg, she leaned back against the seat and closed her eyes.

She had almost kissed him. Almost kissed Logan Burkett. And yet she hadn't given him a copy of Rico's New Testament.

Her phone jangled, causing her to jump again. Though she did not recognize the number, Pippa answered, her hands shaking.

A few minutes later she had what she thought might be another answer to prayer. Or it was the worst idea ever.

A quick text to Rico asking him to meet her at the skate park and she backed out of the parking space in front of the Branson Building. The chandelier glittered on the second floor, but the quick glace she gave as she drove away did not reveal any view of Logan or his father.

When she got back to R10:14, she found Rico already inside waiting for her. "That was fast," she said.

"I was already here," he answered. "Figured I'd get some painting done while the place was empty." He nodded to the corner of the warehouse where a spotlight had been clamped to a ladder to provide light for a large piece of wood.

"What are you working on?"

He showed her and she smiled. "You've got such talent," she said. "I hope you do something with this someday."

Rico shrugged. "It's just a hobby. I really want to go to seminary."

She patted the young man's shoulder. "I know. You'd make an excellent preacher."

His tolerance of praise was less than his tolerance of misbehavior among the kids who skated here. He shook his head. "So, I got your text. What's up?"

"Well," she said, "you know I was able to book the band I told you about for the Memorial Day Bash."

"Awesome."

"Well, it gets better."

Rico leaned against the ladder. "How so?"

"They're willing to play the festival for a low fee, and they're bringing along another Christian band as a warm-up act." Pippa interrupted Rico's low whistle with a sweep of her hand. "There's more. They will sponsor T-shirts for the participants and they want to pay for another print run of the New Testaments with your artwork on them."

Rico laughed out loud. "Wait. Are you serious?"

"Completely." She paused to take a breath and let it out slowly. "But there's more."

His look bade her to continue.

"The group wants to use our warehouse to shoot a music video." She paused. "This coming weekend."

"What?" he said under his breath.

"I know." Pippa wrapped her hands around her waist and allowed her gaze to sweep across the meager interior. "On top of all that, they want to incorporate information about our ministry into the video." She shook her head. "I just can't believe it."

And then Rico began to laugh again. "Oh, Flip, don't you see what this means?"

She returned her attention to the skater. "I can see a lot of things this might mean."

"'How, then, can they call on the one they have not believed in?'" Rico said. "'And how can they believe in the one of whom they have not heard? And how can they hear without someone preaching to them?' Romans 10:14, Flip." He paused. "We get to tell them. This video will let us tell them."

"So you're for it?"

"Have you been listening? Yes, I am for it. Not only that, but I've been praying for something like this to happen. Well, that's not true."

"No?"

"No, my faith was far too small to imagine anything like this."

Pippa nodded. "Then I'm going to text you the contact number for the band's manager. I told them you were the one they needed to talk to."

Rico laughed. "Since when?"

"Since you know the heart of this ministry and what it takes to reach kids. I trust you, Rico," she said. "However, the only way I will sign off on this deal is that I get veto power over everything. Got it?"

"Yes, ma'am!"

She copied the number and sent it to Rico. "All right. The manager's name is Bryan Feldman. He's expecting to hear from you."

Rico started to make the call and Pippa stopped him. "Use my office." She shook her head. "Our office. You'll find there's a spare notepad and pens in the top left drawer of the desk in case you need to take notes."

She watched Rico jog toward the office. Just before he reached the door he jumped to touch the door frame as if he were making a slam-dunk move on the basketball court. A loud whoop punctuated the move and echoed in the cavernous space.

A moment later Pippa heard him clear his throat. "Yes, Mr. Feldman. This is Rico. That is, this is Richard Galvan. Miss Gallagher informed me you would be expecting my call."

His formality made her smile, as did the authoritative way the young man took charge of the call.

Pippa's phone rang. Logan. She let it go to voice mail. One thing at a time, and right now she could not deal with the consequences of a near kiss when the future of the ministry was being discussed in the next room.

A buzz indicated Logan had left a message. She resisted checking to see what he'd said. She could do that later.

Rico's laughter drifted through the open door.

Yes, she would listen to that message later.

Chapter Fourteen

Logan dropped the phone back into his pocket and leaned against the window. The potential buyer for the machine shop had lowered his bid and wasn't budging. The amount was an insult, and yet Logan was considering the offer anyway.

Anything to get that last tie to Ashley severed.

The Starting Over guys had set the date for the neighborhood cleanup. He called Dad back and told him the date, giving him the suggestion to let the potential buyer know the neighborhood would look different if he would just wait a few days.

"I'll try," Dad said, although Logan knew from his tone that his father didn't hold out much hope of a higher offer.

Outside, the rain still pelted the windows, and it looked as if the storm wasn't going anywhere for hours. Logan went downstairs to retrieve his tool belt and then set to work on the framing he'd promised Pippa he could do today. His heart wasn't in it.

But then his heart had walked out the door with Pippa Gallagher an hour ago.

Or rather run.

When his phone rang again a while later, Logan nearly dropped the hammer on his foot in his haste to grab the call. "More news," his dad said.

"What's that?" Logan tried not to sound disappointed. "Did the buyer come back with a better offer after all?"

"No, but I do have someone else interested."

"Oh?"

"Guy from Houston who's looking to retire out our way. He thinks he may be able to get down here and see the place in the next week or so." He paused. "You don't sound happy. Have you changed your mind about selling?"

"Since we talked an hour ago? No." Logan let out a long breath. "Sorry, Dad. I'm very glad to hear this. Any idea whether this one's going to try and lowball us on the selling price, too?"

"I suppose that's always a possibility, but so is the idea that these potential buyers could get caught up in a bidding war. Remember, our current fellow knows there are no other bids, and he can see from the Multiple Listing Service report that the property has been sitting on the market for a few months."

"True."

"Likely he thinks he's sitting in the catbird's seat just waiting until we agree to his terms. I predict he will show his hand once he knows there's another offer on the table."

"I'll hang on to that possibility. Just see if you can get him to wait until after the cleanup." When his father did not respond, Logan continued. "Dad? Was there something else?"

"Tell me it's none of my business, but did I walk in on something between you and Pippa Gallagher?"

Logan tightened his grip on the phone. "I don't know.

And that's the best answer I can give you." His laughter held no humor. "I wish I knew."

"Uh-oh."

"What?"

"Well," Dad said, "I didn't want to tell you this when I was there, but what I saw when I walked into that loft was a woman looking at a man like she had fallen for him. And, son, you had that same look."

"Yeah, I probably did."

"Well, one of these days you'll know for sure. And in the meantime you know where to go to get guidance. Besides to me, that is."

Logan did. "Yeah, Dad. The Lord and I have been having regular conversations. Here lately most of them have been about Pippa Gallagher."

"Glad to hear it," Dad said a bit too quickly.

"Are you, now?" Logan paused. "And why is that? You haven't bought into Eric's girls' matchmaking, have you?"

"Total nonsense," his father said. "Well, other than the fact that they set Eric and Amy off on the path that led to marriage. You know that story, don't you?"

Logan smiled. "Yeah. Daddy's little matchmakers had some help from your wife, if I recall. Isn't she the one who made it possible for them to advertise in the newspaper for a mom?"

"That's the story I got," he said. "But you have my word there will be no newspaper articles about you and Pippa. I'll make sure Susan knows that's not going to work this time around."

"Dad."

"Oh, come on, son. It's a joke."

"I know," Logan finally said. "It's just that…"

What? That his attachment to Pippa had taken him

by surprise? That he had never had such a tangle of deep emotions for a woman, not even Ashley?

"That you've got it bad and don't know what to do about it?"

"No." Logan paused. "Yeah, maybe. I just… Well, I wasn't looking to have any feelings for her, but then they kind of snuck up on me."

"Then I guess the next question I would ask is what are you planning to do about those sneaky feelings?"

Good question. "I don't know."

"Does she have feelings for you?"

"I don't know that, either."

"Well," his father said slowly, "I would say that's the first thing you need to find out. Then you can decide what your next step is."

Leave it to Dad to come up with the most obvious and yet the least practical solution. Logan went back to work framing up the pantry. Determining to keep at the job until Pippa called him back, he finally quit a few hours later when his stomach complained that it was time for dinner.

As Logan turned off the lights and let himself out of the building, he dodged the raindrops to climb inside the Jeep. The windows down the street at Gallagher and Company were dark, so he knew Pippa wasn't still at work.

He debated driving by Pippa's place to see if she was home. Maybe check on whether she had seen his message.

A horn honked and a dark blue pickup truck pulled up beside him, the Vine Beach city seal emblazoned on the door along with the words Fire Marshal. Ryan Owen lowered the window and nodded.

"I kept waiting for the rain to stop so I could come

over and see the progress," Ryan said. "Leah's been telling me about the renovation. It's got her champing at the bit to start on Berryhill."

"I'm sure," Logan said. "Would you like to come in and see the place?"

Ryan waved away the question with a sweep of his hand. "Thanks, but I'll take a rain check if you're offering them. Pardon the pun. Leah's got the night off from the Seafood Shack and I promised I'd come home early."

"Absolutely."

"The other thing I was wondering…" Ryan paused a second. "I know you're working for the Gallagher ladies for now, but I wonder if you've ever considered doing restoration work elsewhere." Another pause. "Like Berryhill?"

"Wow." Logan chewed on that thought a second. "I don't know. I mean yeah, that's definitely something that I'd like to talk more about."

"I saw what you did for Eric and Amy. I know you do good work." He nodded to the Branson Building. "And you don't mind working with the historical commission folks, which is one nightmare I don't even want to try to handle. Forget about it." Ryan paused. "And I'm the fire marshal. If anyone knows about red tape and paperwork, it's me."

Logan joined his laughter. "They're nice enough folks. You just have to learn to speak their language. Haven't had any trouble with them while I've been working on the Branson Building. Or I guess it's technically the Gallagher Building now."

"And that, my friend, is why I have chosen to delegate that part of the restoration project." Ryan shrugged. "For that matter, it's all going through Leah anyway. Not only was it her family home, but also she's the expert. I will just be there to make certain the place isn't lost to another fire."

Logan thought of the night the grand home had burned to the ground. "An important job," he said.

"Yes, well, anyway, I'm heading home. Guessing you're doing the same."

"Yeah, home."

But as Ryan drove away, Logan was struck by the fact that he really didn't feel as if he had a home anymore. It wasn't Zambia and it certainly wasn't Alaska. The place he lived now was nice but Spartan enough to offer nothing but the basics of comfort plus a giant television for college football Saturdays.

But it wasn't a home. Nor was the place Dad and Susan lived, although he knew he was always welcome there.

The last time he felt at home? Logan thought a minute. That would have been just a few days ago when he sat on Pippa's rented porch and drank iced tea in the moonlight.

Logan pointed the Jeep down Main Street until it intersected with Vine Beach Highway. The rain had tapered off, leaving a shimmer on the road and the occasional splat of raindrops on his windshield.

A right turn would take him back to his place, a left turn led to Pippa's. When the light turned green, he hesitated only a second. Then he turned left.

The distance to Pippa's place was measured in minutes not miles, and he arrived at her driveway just a few minutes later. Unfortunately two other vehicles had beat him to it. While he didn't recognize the black Hummer with the rims and darkened windows, he would know the other car any day.

It belonged to his demo guy. What were Rico Galvan and some dude with a Hummer doing at Pippa's place?

* * *

Pippa signed her name on the contract and then looked across the table at Bryan Feldman. "It's a skate park where kids come and go. That's our ministry. If we close down and have things going on inside, the kids are going to wonder what's happening."

"I understand, but you need to see our position in this. If Romans Ten is going to make a splash with their first record, we need a killer video. To have a killer video, we need—"

"To have complete control of the environment through an exclusivity agreement," Pippa supplied. "Yes, I know."

"I know in a town this size the secret's going to be hard to hide, but it's just for the rest of the week." The band manager shrugged. "I've found that once people realize you've made their town famous, they are extremely forgiving about being kept in the dark about it."

"Yes, but my concern is the kids."

"Maybe I can set up an alternative place to gather," Rico said. "I could talk to Chief Owen. He's got a sweet place out in the country with—"

"No." Pippa tempered her response. "If we start involving other people, directly or indirectly, then it becomes more difficult to keep everything under wraps."

Brian gave a reassuring nod. "I think it would be safe to say that the building is undergoing some renovations and let the details be a mystery. How does that sound?"

Pippa still doubted they could get away with the diversion. Then she thought of the neighborhood cleanup coming in a few days. Perhaps that activity would keep the kids busy enough not to miss skating afterward.

Even as she considered the idea, she didn't believe it would work.

"It's true, Flip." Rico shrugged. "Between the work

they'll have me doing to bring the inside up to what they want and the new ramps they're going to be leaving behind, I'd call those 'renovations.'"

"All right," Pippa said, "but what about the music itself? Will the band actually be playing during the days you're using the space?"

"That's the plan, though I'll have to speak to our production guy to get the exact schedule. I've explained to Mr. Galvan that we will need a key holder on the premises at all times."

"And I have explained that he's the one you will be dealing with most of the time. I'm just the one with the veto power." They shared a laugh and then someone knocked. "That's strange."

Pippa rose. "I'll just go see who it is. Rico, why don't you show Mr. Feldman the sketches you came up with this afternoon for the artwork they want on the walls?"

Pippa peered out the window and spied Logan standing on the porch. "Oh, no."

"What is it?" Bryan called.

"A friend of mine," she said. "I can't ignore him. He knows I'm home."

Rico looked up from his sketches. "If you need to talk to the guy, go ahead."

She looked to Bryan, who nodded. "All right, but I'll just be outside if you need me."

"And remember," Bryan said, "you're under contract not to say a word about this. I don't care how good a friend the person is. One word and the deal is off."

Great. Not telling Logan felt too close to lying for comfort, but it *was* just temporary. Surely he would understand when she finally was free to explain.

Logan knocked again, and this time Pippa opened the door and slipped outside. "Logan," she said as remnants from the day's rain dripped off the eaves and slid down her back. "What are you doing here?"

"I, uh, that is, I was driving home and I wondered if you…" He shook his head and looked past her to the door and then returned his focus to Pippa. "I called you earlier. Left a message."

"Oh, no." Pippa sighed. In all the excitement she had completely forgotten to return his call. Or to listen to his message. "Oh, Logan, I'm so sorry. See, something came up and I couldn't answer when you called. Business stuff. And then other stuff happened and I had…"

"Stuff to do?" he supplied.

Another raindrop snaked down her spine, and she suppressed a chill. "Yes, something like that."

Men's laughter drifted through the door to slide past them, and Pippa cringed. "Um, Logan, why don't we go downstairs? There's a swing under the carport where we can sit."

Pippa pressed past him to the stairs. He nodded but made no move to follow her. "Are you coming?" she finally asked.

"Yeah, sure."

Logan had barely had time to settle beside her when he looked up at the rafters as the creak of heavy footsteps sounded overhead. The swing was hung below the kitchen. Rico was probably filling water glasses. But she couldn't tell Logan that, could she?

"Okay, so I came here to talk to you, but I'm not going to ignore the fact that a black Hummer and my demo guy's car are in your driveway and, unless I miss my guess, they are having a grand time upstairs in your kitchen."

"Yes," she said slowly, "that's true. And though I know you're too polite to ask, I have to tell you that I'm not able to answer any questions about what they're doing or why they're meeting here. I can tell you that nothing's going on that would be considered illegal and that it has to do with something that only God could bring about."

"I see."

Pippa swiveled to face him. "Logan, I'm so sorry. It's a meeting about a ministry. I probably shouldn't tell you that much, and I really want to say more, but I just can't. It's important that you trust me."

Another squeak above their heads reminded them they were not completely alone. "Okay," he said. "Look, I shouldn't have come here tonight. I'm just going to go now."

Logan started to stand and Pippa reached to grasp his elbow. "Please don't."

A shrug.

"Not yet."

"But…" He nodded to the driveway. "Don't your guests need you?"

"I told you, Logan. It's a ministry thing. I'm just providing a place for them to meet, that's all."

Rather than return to the swing, Logan pulled her to her feet. "Okay, look. I'll just say it. I don't know what got into me today. Back at the jobsite, I mean. One minute we were having a conversation about French doors and the next I almost…"

"Kissed me?" Pippa met his gaze. "You're not about to apologize for that, are you? Because then you will have something to make amends for."

He smiled. "Hardly."

And then he kissed her.

Chapter Fifteen

He kissed her.

Logan woke up the next morning sure the whole thing was a dream. And then, as he slowly came awake, he knew it was no dream.

Had he any remains of good sense, he might have stuck around and actually had a conversation with Pippa about feelings and relationships and the like. But with the mystery meeting going on upstairs, any declarations of that sort had to be put on hold.

If he decided to state his case, he would do it at a time when somebody else was walking around in Pippa's kitchen. Logan rose and checked his emails.

Though he found several from contractors regarding the Gallagher project, he saw nothing from the lovely Miss Gallagher herself. No texts, either. Or phone messages.

What was she doing this morning? Was she up early or was she, too, just waking up and thinking about the kiss?

Logan padded to the bathroom and reached for toothbrush and toothpaste. The man in the mirror had it bad.

And he wouldn't have it any other way.

His phone buzzed, and Logan nearly broke his neck

tripping over his work boots to get to it. A text from his father. Reminding you Susan and I are leaving this morning on our golf trip. Be back Sunday night. Will share any information on situation with property as it happens.

Logan sent back a quick response and then got on with preparing for his day. Once in his truck, as he threw his tool belt onto the front seat, he spied the sweatshirt Pippa had returned and grinned.

This morning his drive took him out to see Joey at the salvage yard for some pieces he'd forgotten to include in his delivery. As he left, Logan spied the rusted phone box and shook his head. On the way back into town, he drove past Berryhill, or at least where Berryhill would one day stand again.

Maybe he would think a little harder about being part of that restoration. It would certainly give him a reason to stick around Vine Beach a little longer. Or, with a project of this size, a lot longer.

And it interested him. Rebuilding a home from the ashes. Making something from nothing. Yes, that got his blood stirring.

Maybe there was something of an architect in him after all.

Two days later, Logan met the Starting Over guys at the church and helped load supplies for the neighborhood cleanup. When the trucks arrived at the neighborhood, he spied Pippa and her crew waiting for them. Dad and Eric drove up as the guys were unloading the equipment.

"Everyone know their assignments?" Logan called when all the participants had gathered around.

"We don't," Pippa said.

"Some of you can work with us," Eric called as he reached for several garden implements. "I'm in charge of turning that pile of weeds across the street into a late summer garden."

Several of the skaters hurried over to grab rakes and hoes. The rest hung back and seemed to be waiting for Pippa to reply. Or maybe they were standing guard in case she needed them. A second look at the ragtag bunch, and Logan decided it was definitely the latter.

"What about some painting?" Logan said with a grin. Before Pippa could respond, he hurried to add, "The signs over at Taylor Trucking are barely readable, and their office's front doors could use some varnish."

"I'll take that job."

Logan looked behind him to see his demo guy walking toward him. "Hey, Rico. Didn't expect to see you here."

The kid exchanged glances with Pippa and then returned his attention to Logan. "Guess I should have told you before now, but I'm one of them." He nodded toward Pippa and her crew. "I'm a skater."

Logan thought a minute and then shrugged. "Well, then, skater. Want to paint the signs or the doors?"

"All of them." Rico pointed toward Pippa. "You need any of these slackers or can I take them?"

"They're all yours," Pippa said. "Just make sure you stick to the same design on the new signs that was on the old ones."

Rico laughed. By the time he stopped in front of Logan, his smile was gone. "Am I still working for you?" he asked, his gaze never wavering.

So the kid thought he'd fire him once he found out about his skating? It took Logan a second to get past that. Was he that awful?

Slowly he extended his hand and shook Rico's. "You are," he said. "Unless you've got a better offer that I don't know about. And in that case, I'll see if I can't match the salary."

Rico laughed again. "You pay me fine, sir. However, if I get into the seminary, the deal is off."

Seminary? Logan quickly shook off his surprise. "If you get into seminary, I'll be glad to see you go. Otherwise, I'll expect you at work like always."

"Yes, sir." Rico glanced back at his team. "Come on. Let's get this done."

Logan watched the demo guy bark orders as he crossed the street and headed down toward Taylor Trucking. The kid was a natural leader.

"That was a nice thing you just did."

Logan turned his attention to Pippa, who now stood beside him. She'd tamed her golden hair beneath a yellow baseball cap and wore cutoff jeans and a T-shirt, but she was still the prettiest girl he'd ever seen. A swift memory of several kisses rose. He pushed it away.

"It was good business," Logan insisted. "Rico's a hard worker."

Pippa gave him a look. "True."

Logan surveyed the street. The painters seemed to be settling in, and just next door to the trucking company, the gardeners were busy taming the plot of weeds. Several other groups were in the process of tearing down the abandoned buildings that were slated for demolition.

He turned back to Pippa. "There are two jobs left."

"Doesn't matter which one," she said. "Just give me an assignment."

"All right." Logan went around to the back of the truck and pulled out another gallon of paint and two brushes. After pretending to walk toward the skate park, he hung a quick right and stopped next door at a wide wooden fence. Behind the fence was a conglomeration of electrical equipment belonging to the city and to the telephone company. At one time, the fence had probably been a good way to hide an eyesore. Now it was an eyesore itself.

"Very funny," Pippa said as she caught up to him.

"Just teasing." He nodded toward the brightly painted building. "Unless you'd like to start over there first."

Pippa gave him a playful swat with the dry brush, then stepped back and watched while he opened the paint can and gave the liquid inside a stir. An hour later, they'd covered a good expanse of the fence with bright white paint. They'd also dotted themselves with the same color.

Logan leaned over to swipe at a dot of paint on Pippa's cheek and then stole a kiss. When she didn't protest, he did it again.

"At this rate, we will never get this fence painted," she said with a giggle.

He lifted one eyebrow as if he were considering the statement. Then he kissed her again.

"Logan Burkett!" she exclaimed. "Behave yourself."

"Listen to the lady," Dad said, causing Logan to jump and sending a splatter of white paint down the front of Dad's favorite green golf shirt.

"Oh, Dad. Sorry about that."

His father's gaze shifted from him to Pippa. Both seemed to be having trouble keeping a straight face.

"All right," Logan said. "Enough of you two. Two of us need to get back to painting and the other should go and check on the kids over at Taylor Trucking."

Dad shrugged. "Well, since you two work so well together, why don't I just go on down the street and leave you to your work?"

"Good idea," Logan managed.

"Not nearly as good an idea as the one you had to finally kiss that girl," he said over his shoulder as he hurried away.

"He's incorrigible," Pippa said. "I see where you get it from."

"Me?"

She nudged his shoulder and then went back to painting. Logan did the same, although he sent more than a few glances in her direction when he could manage them.

By the time the church ladies arrived to set up tables under the awning of the machine shop and then load them up with enough lunch items to feed an army, Logan had given up hiding how much he was beginning to care for the girl who ran the skating ministry.

Now if he could only figure out what to do about it.

The question lingered in Logan's mind well past the moment he watched Pippa drive away, shuttling three of the skaters home. He leaned against his Jeep, even after her car disappeared around the corner, and wondered why he had fallen for a woman who had such different ideas from his.

And yet they were very much alike in many ways. They had a shared history on the missions field, hers as a child and his more recent. Both of them worried for the future of Vine Beach's youth. Surely those things were enough to form some kind of middle ground between them.

A hand clasped Logan's shoulder, and he turned around to see a few of the Starting Over guys standing there. "Lost in thought?" one of them asked.

"Guess I was," Logan said. "So, great day, wasn't it?"

Just like that, the conversation turned to the progress they had made in turning a dead-end street into a neighborhood on the mend. The folks at Taylor Trucking were so thankful they made a sizable donation to the Starting Over fund, something Logan announced at the next regular meeting of the widowers group.

As the applause died down, Logan returned to his seat. The group that once had Dad at the helm and his stepbrother, Eric, as a member still met on Saturday mornings to play basketball and provide support to men who found themselves mourning their wives. Some were older, while many were Logan's age. A few were younger.

Some lost their spouses to cancer, others to war. Others, like Logan, had become widowers because of accidents. As far as he knew, he was the only one who was directly responsible for the events that caused his wife to die.

Then a man named Ken stood to tell his story. Ken was new to the group, just moved from Houston down to the beach to retire. He was near Dad's age and graying at the temples, his face lined with years and, as his story began to unfold, obviously with grief.

Logan listened to the tale, his fingers gripping the sides of his chair until he no longer felt them. Ken and his wife had argued about something so inconsequential that he couldn't recall what it was. But life had been reduced to that kind of nitpicking between them, this being just one in a long line of disagreements. This time, however, when she threatened to leave, he called her bluff. Helped her pack. All the time thinking she would be back before dark.

But she didn't come back. Pride kept Ken waiting until morning to go searching for her, but no one had seen her. Assuming family was hiding her, he went home and returned to the regular rhythms of his life: work, home, church. All the while Ken kept a watchful eye on the door thinking she would come back. Kept calling her phone thinking she would answer. A month went by. He filed a police report. Then another month and another. Then came the news. His wife had never made it out of their neighborhood. Such was her upset that she drove her car off a bridge into a drainage ditch where it had been hidden under the water. The car and her remains were found when the swollen creek dried up during a summer drought.

"So learn from me," Ken said. "Never let words go unsaid or actions go undone. You can't know whether any conversation might be your last."

Few in the crowd appeared untouched by the man's story. Logan swiped at tears as their leader led the group in a parting prayer. *Never let words go unsaid or actions go undone.* As he left the meeting, Logan made himself and God a promise that he would live by those words. His first stop was Dad's office, where he was putting in a few extra hours on a Saturday morning.

"Glad to see you, son," his father said.

Logan bypassed the greeting to offer his dad a hug.

"What was that for?" he asked when Logan stepped back.

He shrugged. "Just wanted to thank you, Dad," he said. "For all you've done to make me the man I am."

His father was still smiling when Logan left a few minutes later. Logan's next stop was the Branson Building and the nearby offices Gallagher and Company, where he hoped he would find Pippa's car out front. When he saw she wasn't at either location, he picked up the phone and called her.

On the fourth ring, her voice mail picked up. "This is Logan," he said. "Call me when you can. I just want to hear your voice."

And to tell you what I have been leaving unsaid.

Chapter Sixteen

Pippa shook her head. "Absolutely not."

Monday morning dawned early and with it, the beginning of a week of filming at R10:14. The crew had arrived well before daylight, quickly turning the sparsely furnished but tidy warehouse space into a tangle of wires, lights and other pieces of equipment. Rico's banners were being hung as fast as he could paint them, and though the space had been ventilated, the smell of spray paint hung heavy in the air.

Bryan Feldman had exchanged last night's business casual attire for running shoes, cargo shorts and a T-shirt with the band's signature logo emblazoned across a field of pearl white. His hands were stuffed into the front pockets, only his Rolex watch and the strands of silver in his hair and goatee giving away the fact that he wasn't one of them.

Stretching out the kinks from muscles that were still complaining after the neighborhood cleanup, Pippa turned her attention to the man who would be producing the video.

"Surely you cannot believe that filming me on a skateboard would be remotely interesting."

"It's not required," Bryan said. "But think of the power that scene would add to the video."

"Come on, Flip!" Rico urged from his place at the canvas. "How many kids are going to see anyone land a crazy trick on the ramps, much less the lady in charge of things at the ministry? I'm with Mr. Feldman. Think of the power."

"I'm thinking of the bruises," Pippa quipped as she recalled her less than dignified landing the last time she attempted the skating trick. "And the blooper reel."

Before Bryan could respond, the big warehouse door rolled open and a bearded guy carrying a snare drum stepped inside. "I'm with the band," he called.

It quickly became apparent he was one of four similarly dressed twentysomethings who made up Romans Ten. After introductions, the foursome got to work placing their equipment in various spots around the warehouse. With each placement, Bryan would snap a photograph with his phone and send it off to the film crew.

Pippa took advantage of the distraction to retreat to her office and close the door. Moving a box of banners advertising the Memorial Day Bash off her chair, she settled down to call Logan.

He picked up on the second ring. "I'm sorry I missed your call," she said. "I didn't see your message until this morning."

"Yeah?"

"Yeah." She thought of his simple but insistent request that she call him back. That he just needed to hear her voice. "And I needed to hear your voice." Hammering and the banter of male voices sounded in the background. Logan must be at the building supervising some sort of work. "But you're busy."

"Come by and see me later?"

Someone knocked and Pippa rose to walk toward the door. "Will you be at the building for a while?"

"It should be a long day. Between the tile guys working on the marble in the kitchen and the bathroom and the crew fitting in the staircase, we're going to be at this for hours." He paused. "Then there's this crazy assignment I'm working on—putting a computer workstation into a shrunken-down phone booth."

Rico gestured that Pippa was needed over at the ramp. Crew members were hotly debating something, and a man holding an 8 mm camera on his shoulder stood capturing the scene. Pippa nodded and then held up her index finger to let him know she would be there in a minute.

"It's a proper British phone box, thank you very much," she said when she had turned her back on the chaos in the warehouse. "From what I've been reading, it's probably a prop for a movie or a play that was made to the scale needed." She paused. "Or maybe it just shrank."

They shared a laugh and then someone called Logan's name. "I should go see about that."

"Yes. You do that."

"But first…"

Pippa leaned against the edge of the desk. "Yes?"

"About those kisses?" he said.

"Yes?"

His chuckle was deep and low. "I'm still not sorry."

"Neither am I," she said as she hung up and tucked the phone into her pocket, then grabbed a box of Rico's New Testaments and walked toward the ramp.

"Here she is," Bryan called.

Suddenly all eyes were pointed at Pippa. Even the cameraman swung his attention and the camera in her direction. Someone adjusted a spotlight to point at her, flooding her face with heat and light.

Rico made the introductions: four band members, three electricians, a lighting guy and a cameraman. "Only one camera so it feels like the movies we take of ourselves when we're skating," he continued as the others nodded.

"Well, it's very nice to meet all of you. And thank you," she said to the members of Romans Ten. "Your generous donation is going to make for a great Memorial Day Bash for our kids. May I reciprocate with these?" She nodded to Rico and he took the books to pass out to the group.

While comments on the art vied with words of thanks, Pippa took a moment to allow her gaze to sweep around the room. With Rico's banners hanging behind the ramp, the place looked like a proper skate park.

Bryan caught her staring and went to stand beside her. "Your kid is brilliant," he said. "Not only does his art capture the feel of skating, but he also uses biblical elements. It's just amazing." He gestured to a panel more than six feet wide and at least eight feet long. While a casual onlooker might see what appeared to be graffiti, a closer look revealed the text of Joshua 1:9: *Have I not commanded you? Be strong and courageous. Do not be afraid. Do not be discouraged. For the Lord your God will be there with you wherever you go.*

"Brilliant," the manager said again. "I'd like to represent him."

"What?" Pippa jerked her attention to Bryan. "But he's a painter. Who wants to be a preacher, by the way."

Bryan nodded thoughtfully. "He's an artist called by God."

"Yes, he is," she said.

"I'm just the guy who can handle the details." Bryan paused. "I understand you have veto power."

Pippa looked over at Rico. "Only with the ministry. What Rico does is up to him."

"Good," Bryan said. "Now, about the skating trick we'll be filming."

"Bryan," she said slowly, "I never agreed to that."

He took a step back and crossed his arms over his chest. "Interesting."

"What?"

The manager shook his head. "I thought I was looking at someone who would do almost anything for her ministry. Funny, but I seem to recall you saying those exact words."

He had her there.

An idea occurred. "All right, I'll do it but only on one condition."

A sideways look. "And that would be?"

Pippa smiled. "I don't know yet. But I have a feeling I'm going to need something someday and you just might be the guy to call."

Bryan stuck out his hand. "Deal." They shook and then he pulled out his business card. "Got a pen?"

"Somebody need a pen?" Rico called as he came walking over with a marker. "How's this?"

"Perfect. Now turn around. I need a portable writing desk." Rico complied and Bryan placed the business card against Rico's back and wrote something on it. "Here you go, Miss Flip."

She accepted the card and read the note. *Owed to Flip Gallagher one favor. Payable upon presentation.* "That's quite formal," she said.

Bryan laughed and then glanced over his shoulder. "Prep the ramp for the McTwist shot," he called.

Pippa tucked the card into her pocket. "Now?"

He shrugged. "Why not? What you're wearing is fine."

She looked down at her faded jeans and favorite Romans 10:14 T-shirt. Further preparation wouldn't make her any better, and thinking about it would only frazzle her nerves. "Oh, why not?"

A few minutes later, she came out of the office with her helmet and pads. The cell phone she left on her desk began to ring, and Pippa almost turned around to grab it. But she'd just spoken with Logan. Any delay of this stunt and she might not go through with it.

The ringing chased her across the warehouse until it finally stopped. Meanwhile the lighting guy was setting up tripods and the band members had busied themselves arranging their instruments in front of the ramp. Apparently Romans Ten would be playing its future hit song while she skated.

Great.

And yet she had given her word.

"Okay," Pippa said on a long release of breath. "I'm ready for my close-up, Mr. DeMille."

"Uh, ma'am," the drummer called, "his name is Chaz."

"Right." Pippa turned to find the man in question had his camera poised just inches from her face. "Okay, let's do this, Chaz."

He grinned and peered from around the antique 8 mm camera. "Hey, I kind of liked being called Mr. DeMille."

"Make me look good and I'll call you whatever you want." Pippa laughed. "And if you edit out the part where I fall on my face, I'll be eternally grateful."

"I'll see what I can do, Flip. Now go break a leg." As soon as he said the words, Chaz cringed. "Not appropriate in this context, is it?"

Pippa adjusted the strap on her helmet, then looked back at Chaz. "Um, no."

* * *

Logan tucked the phone back into his shirt pocket and shifted the Jeep into Reverse. Leave it to Dad to be out of town when the buyer who was merely interested became seriously motivated. Logan was no Realtor, but he figured he could show a man around an empty machine shop as well as anyone else.

And the man in question was heading there right now.

If Vine Beach were any bigger, Logan never would have arrived at the machine shop so fast. But thankfully the city had no real traffic except when the Fourth of July parade shut down Main Street or the Friday night football games over at the high school let out.

When he turned onto the street, the first thing he saw was the number of vehicles, including several vans, in the parking lot of the warehouse next door. "Looks like some of the skaters have learned to drive," he mumbled.

He spied a moving truck among them. Odd but Pippa hadn't mentioned anything going on at the building that would require a truck. Logan made a note to go and check out what was happening after he met with the buyer.

A black sedan pulled in beside him, and the driver rolled down the window. "Burkett?"

"Yes, and you must be Sam Clark," Logan said as he climbed out and went around to shake hands with the older gentleman. "Come with me and I will show you around, sir."

They exchanged pleasantries as Logan retrieved the key to the front door. "The neighborhood looks better than it did online, but that place over there's got funny writing on it," Sam said. "You got a gang problem around here? I won't tolerate gangs."

"No, sir. There are no gangs in Vine Beach." Logan bit back the complaint he could easily have lodged against his neighbor. "Apparently that's what passes for art now-adays."

He jabbed a key into to the lock. Wrong one. Logan tried again.

"Lots of activity," Sam continued. "I see a moving truck. Think maybe they're moving out?"

"Don't know," Logan said as he tried another key.

"Well, if they're moving out, then maybe I'm buy-ing. I like this location and your price is fair. I just won't have any nonsense. The high crime rate is what has me leaving my—"

Suddenly the staccato beat of what sounded like gun-fire erupted. Its source could only be inside the ware-house, for no one else was around. Sam hit the floor, while Logan fumbled the keys.

Before he could retrieve the key ring and help the older gentleman up, someone inside the building began to count. Apparently into a very loud microphone. Or maybe some kind of sound system. Turned to extra loud.

Whatever the source, "And a one, two, three, four" rang out across the neighborhood.

Logan extended his hand to pull Sam Clark up by his elbow. "Here, let me help—"

Then came the guitars, and drums, and more guitars and possibly even a cowbell. Mr. Clark stumbled forward, but Logan caught him.

"What in the world is going on over there?" he asked Logan.

"I need to go find out," he said. "Would you mind waiting here while I do that?"

"I don't believe I'm going to stick around," Mr. Clark said. "I appreciate your showing me the building on short notice, but if this is what it's like in this neighborhood, I think I'll just mosey on back to Houston where it's quieter."

"But honestly, sir. This is the first time I've heard this kind of noise." Other noise, yes, like skaters and a sound system draped over a parking lot sign, but never this. Surely Pippa could offer a reasonable explanation. Still, the timing couldn't be worse.

But Mr. Clark would hear none of it. Instead he peeled out and left skid marks in his wake.

By the time Logan had stuffed his keys back into his pocket and headed toward the warehouse, his only chance of getting a decent price for the machine shop was almost to the highway. He marched across the parking lot, making his way through vans and cars and over what appeared to be a mine field of orange extension cords and cables.

Was that the Hummer he'd seen at Pippa's place? Interesting.

Logan reached for his phone to call the cops and then thought better of it. If what was going on inside had Pippa's approval, he didn't want to cause any trouble for her. Instead he pressed Record and used his phone to sweep the parking lot, capturing license plates and vehicle descriptions as well as the sound of the music inside. Strange, but Pippa's car was not among them.

The closer Logan got, the louder the music blared. At least he didn't have to worry about being quiet and trying to sneak up on them, he thought as he yanked the door open and stepped inside, his phone still recording. The sound hit him first and then the lights all aimed at the center of the room.

As Logan expected, a live band was playing, its lyrics surprisingly Christian in content. Banners were draped from all four walls of the warehouse, all matching the same graffiti style painted on the outside of the building.

Behind the band was a skateboard ramp painted a gar-

ish sunshine yellow. A lone skater sailed down one side
and turned a flip before landing on the other. A cameraman captured each move the dude made while a dozen
other hangers-on stood around and nodded.

The fact that all of this was happening while Pippa
was not at the location spurred him forward. As much
as Logan disagreed with the tactics she employed, he
knew how protective she was of this ministry. From the
looks of the building's exterior, Logan thought it possible that the band assumed the building was abandoned.
If these people were trespassing, he would see that they
left quickly or the authorities would be called.

Then a familiar face parted the crowd. "Rico?"

"Hey, Logan," he thought the kid said, though the
music prevented him from knowing for certain. "Isn't
she great?" he did hear, but only because Rico shouted
it into his ear.

Logan shut off the recorder and stuck his phone back
in his pocket. He'd had enough for now. And as much as
he liked Rico, he hated to send him down with the rest
of this sinking ship.

Unless he had to.

"Isn't who great?" Logan shouted as the guy on the
ramp went airborne, twisting and turning like a cork-
screw independent of the laws of gravity. For a second,
Logan exchanged irritation for admiration as he watched
the skateboarder.

Then the skater looked his way. And appeared to
freeze.

As if in slow motion, the skateboard went one way
and the kid went the other. The music stopped, leaving a shocking silence and his ears ringing. Instinct sent
Logan running toward the ramp, hurdling over cables
and guitar cases.

The skater sat up, seemingly dazed. Slowly he pulled off his helmet just as Logan reached the ramp. Blond hair tumbled down, and wide eyes looked his way.

"Pippa?"

Chapter Seventeen

"Logan?" Pippa scrambled to her knees and then slipped off her elbow pads as she stood.

"What are you doing?" he demanded evenly, his expression stony.

"Hey, man, she couldn't tell you about the movie," Chaz said, the camera still rolling. "Confidentiality agreement and all that stuff, you know."

"All that stuff," Logan echoed, "is not what I'm talking about."

"Dude," one of the crew called, "are we going to shoot that again? Flip totally would have nailed that run if this guy hadn't distracted her."

Logan looked confused. "Who's Flip?"

Someone handed Pippa the skateboard she'd been riding, but she shook her head. "Give me a minute."

Logan's voice was low, tight, his jaw clenched. It didn't take a genius to figure out that Logan Burkett was truly mad. What Pippa couldn't figure was why.

The video. Of course. She hadn't told him. That he thought she was hiding something from him stung almost as much as the bruise surely rising on her backside.

"I planned to tell you as soon as I was able," Pippa said. "About the music video, I mean."

Logan shook his head. "This isn't about skating, Pippa."

"Isn't it?"

Pippa turned her attention to Chaz, who was catching every moment of her humiliation. "Think you might take a break now, Mr. DeMille? Maybe turn that thing off?"

His gaze darted between Pippa and Logan and then slowly he shook his head. Apparently the show was too good to change the channel.

"All right, Logan." Pippa stood on shaking knees and then bent over to slip off one of the kneepads. "Then you're going to have to help me," she said when she'd pulled off the second pad. "Because I can see you're beyond angry."

"No, that's not it at all." Logan stood like a sentry, tall and solid in a sea of grunge-plaid shirts and electronic gear. "Do you have any idea how badly you could have been hurt?"

Pippa bit back laughter that held no humor. "It's just skating. Really, Logan, you're being awfully dramatic."

"Am I?" he shouted, bringing the rest of the activity in the room to a swift halt. "I had no idea any of this was going on. Then I walk in and you're taking risks…" He shook his head. "You could have been seriously injured, Pippa. Do you realize that? And for what? A movie?"

"A video," she corrected. "And you're being overprotective."

"Another reason why I think this place should be closed down. 'Just skating'? It didn't look like that to me."

"You want this place closed down?" Pippa's words were full of astonishment mixed with righteous indignation. "Really?"

"At this moment, yes. Between the sale I just lost and the fact that you could have been hurt…" Logan looked away.

Rico came up behind him. "Might want to chill, man," he said. "Go easy on Flip. She's the glue that keeps this place running."

Had Pippa not been embroiled in a situation that was alternately breaking her heart and making her furious, she might have smiled at Rico's mixed metaphor. Instead she watched Logan offer him a stiff nod and then turn to walk away.

He was halfway to the door before Pippa managed to hobble off the ramp and scramble after him. "Come back here, Logan!" she called. "I didn't kiss you just to let you walk away like that."

"Oh, good one."

Pippa turned to see Chaz behind her. Her look wiped the grin off his face.

Meanwhile Logan was out the door and stalking across the parking lot. She gave chase. "Logan, come back and talk to me. Just tell me what I did that was so… Oh!"

Her foot caught on an orange extension cord and sent her sprawling hands first onto the concrete. This time when she rolled into a sitting position, Logan was standing over her.

Without sparing her a word, he reached down to help her up. She caught his arm and held it. "Talk to me, Logan. Because silence is not fair."

She had him. *That* Pippa could see from the expression on Logan's face.

"All right. Thanks to the circus going on over here, the potential buyer I had for the machine shop is gone. And worse, you're bleeding. Look at your knee. I know you love these kids, but there's got to be a better way to reach them."

"What do you mean by that, Logan?"

Through a clenched jaw he said, "Closing it would certainly keep you safe and give me a chance to sell the property. Admit it. I'm right."

Pippa glared at him. Oh, but he was very, very wrong.

"I know it's just a piece of property to everyone else, but I need that machine shop sold. And you? I need you to understand that I cannot lose you."

Pippa heard the words but couldn't quite reconcile them with the expression on his face. With the anger still riveting his posture.

She realized again that this man dismissed everything she held dear within the walls of R10:14. That he would insist she shut it down. "And I was actually falling in love with you." Pippa turned around to walk back inside, only to realize that at some point during the conversation Chaz had developed a sense of discretion and disappeared. Ignoring curious stares and Rico's calling her name, she stepped into her office and grabbed her phone and bag.

"Flip, you okay?" Rico said as he loped toward her.

"I'm fine." Pippa reached into her bag to dig for her keys. "Lock up, okay? And call me only if you absolutely must have me here." She looked into his concerned face. "Got it?"

"Yeah, I got it, but..." He looked down. "You're bleeding."

"I'm fine. I just need to get out of here for a while." She looked past him to Bryan. "Rico's in charge. See you all tomorrow."

Stepping out into the sunshine, one hand still fishing for keys in the bottom of her bag, Pippa found Logan waiting. She pressed past him. Though she had no car, thanks to the film crew's having picked her up, she felt the walk downtown and to the Gallagher and Company offices was manageable.

Or it would have been had her scraped knee not been an issue. Logan fell into step beside her.

"Just leave, okay? I think we've said all we need to for today."

"You said you were falling in love with me."

Pippa picked up her pace. Now her knee was doing more than just complaining.

Logan stepped in front of her, blocking the way. "Do you think I would have purposefully fallen in love with the woman who could single-handedly ruin any chance I had to cut the last tie to my dead wife and who could be seriously hurt with her antics on a skateboard?"

Pippa stared up at him, hands on her hips and anger now pulsing at her temples. "Now, that's quite the question. Tell me, Logan. What's the answer?"

The answer was yes. The same crazy love-struck feeling jabbed him in the heart even now. But he would get over it. He would have to.

They were obviously not made for each other. God didn't put people together when they couldn't agree about so many things, especially their purposes. Pippa could break her neck on that contraption. He refused to lose another woman he loved.

Logan couldn't meet her gaze, so he glanced down at her knee once more. And while he couldn't fix what was broken between them, he could at least do one thing for her.

Logan picked up her bag and then snagged Pippa's wrist. "Come on. And before you argue, your friend with the camera is back and I'm sure the footage of me throwing you over my shoulder to haul you to my car for some first-aid would make great entertainment."

Pippa looked back to see Chaz wave. "I am only doing this because I've already made a fool of myself."

"Doesn't matter to me why. Now watch your step." Logan led her through the maze of vehicles to the back of his Jeep, where he opened the tailgate, hoisted her up and placed her bag next to her.

Pippa sat right where Logan put her until he retrieved the first-aid kit. Blood had soaked her jeans at the knee and splattered in drops down her leg. No way could he adequately treat the wound through the tear in her jeans.

"Close your eyes."

Of course she ignored him.

"Are you enjoying this? Because I'm not!" he snapped. "Cooperate please."

When she complied, Logan found the scissors and cut away enough material from her jeans to have a decent view at the injury beneath.

"What are you doing?"

Logan swatted her hands away. "You ruined them when you fell. I was just trying to get to the injury. Nasty scrape but you won't need stitches. Now hang on while I pour some peroxide on it."

It hurt, but Pippa took it like a trouper. And even though tears shimmered, none fell. Instead she looked away, her attention focused elsewhere as Logan tended to her injury. Only when he clicked the first-aid kit shut did she spare him a glance.

"Thank you," she said, her voice surprisingly gentle.

With a nod, Logan helped her down and then stowed the first-aid kit. He had already climbed behind the steering wheel when Pippa stepped into view.

"You made a nice speech about what I thought and

didn't think you would do, but when I asked you what the truth was, you didn't answer."

He stared straight ahead. He hadn't answered because he wouldn't.

"Logan?"

When he didn't respond, he thought she might leave. Instead Pippa turned her back on the blasted cameraman, who was still filming, although from a distance.

"All right, have it your way. But there's something you ought to know. Those kisses?" Pippa paused as he looked in her face. "I'm still not sorry even if you are. When you're willing to admit how you feel, I'll be happy to discuss it further."

Pippa stepped back from the Jeep. Logan looked away.

"All right, then," she said evenly. "I'm going back to my life. I suggest you go back to yours."

Pippa felt Logan's eyes on her as she straightened her back and walked away, leaving him sitting in the Jeep. She'd managed not to cry while he was working on her leg, and she wouldn't cry now, either.

"And she's back. Did you change your mind about seeing us tomorrow?" Bryan hurried toward her, obviously taking in her bandaged knee and altered jeans. "Oh, no!"

"I'm fine," she said wearily. "And yes, I changed my mind. Going home doesn't sound as appealing as it did before."

Not when she'd have too much to think about and nothing to offer a distraction.

"I'm sure you are, but we can't reshoot the scene. Your jeans are torn and bloody, so they won't look the same as the previous footage."

Chaz slid up beside them. "How about I shoot her doing the McTwist at the festival?"

"Might as well shoot me now," she said. "Just kidding. I won't be doing the McTwist at the Memorial Day Bash. I'm distracted enough with just the band and crew in the room. No way could I do that in front of a big crowd."

"How about before?" Chaz offered. "Early that morning or even the night before when everyone is setting up?"

"I like it," Bryan said. "Pippa?"

"I'll think about it. So, how much longer will you be filming today, Chaz?" she asked.

He shrugged. "Thinking I've got plenty for now. We can knock off anytime. Maybe start up again tomorrow morning."

"Sounds good." Bryan called for attention and the room fell silent. "It's a wrap for today. Get everything packed up into the trucks."

"All of it?" one of the crew called.

"All of it. No offense to Miss Gallagher, but there's not a big enough lock on this place to convince me to keep a half million dollars' worth of equipment in it overnight."

"Nor would I want you to," Pippa said.

"Rico, are those banners dry? I want to roll them up and stick them in the truck just in case. I've got a couple of ideas for some still shots that we may be able to accomplish back at the hotel. Just some promo stuff with the band. If you're all right with your work being used as a backdrop."

"Sure," Rico said enthusiastically.

The men walked away chatting, so Pippa once again headed for her office. Despite efforts to the contrary, the quiet of the room started her thinking about Logan. About their trip to Galveston and the surrey ride. And the kisses.

She had to talk to him. Tomorrow when they both

cooled down, maybe they could look at today in a different light.

Maybe all was not lost.

Pippa hid out in her office until the last cable was wound and removed. Finally the warehouse looked its sparse self again. And tomorrow they would put it all back and film some more.

What a way to make a living.

She bade Chaz and Bryan goodbye and then waited for Rico to get his paints before locking the door. The sun was an orange mist sliding beneath a stripe of gray clouds, and the air felt heavy with humidity.

"Some crazy day," Rico said. "Did you ever think we'd be doing anything like this?"

She smiled. "No, but it was pretty cool, wasn't it?"

"More than cool, Flip," he said. "Too bad your boyfriend messed up your trick."

"He's not my boyfriend," Pippa said.

"Yeah, right," Rico answered as he stowed his paints in the trunk of his sedan.

"Instead of dropping me at home," she said when he joined her in the car, "would you mind taking me to the Gallagher and Company office?"

"Not at all." A few minutes later, she climbed out and told Rico goodbye.

Instead of going inside, Pippa walked down to the Branson Building thinking to look in and check the day's progress. Instead she wandered around the big empty space, alternating between marveling at the beauty of the work the men had done and allowing the feeling of loss to nearly topple her.

On the second floor, she turned on the iron chandelier and gasped. The place looked almost move-in ready. Pages of diagrams lay across the kitchen countertop, the first one showing how to turn the phone box into a computer workstation. Pippa's smile felt bittersweet.

Next she turned to the staircase that Logan's crew had installed and anchored beside what would soon be the new pantry. The spare French door leaned against the wall, its doorknob removed and in pieces on the counter and a fresh coat of lacquer protecting the patina of its aged finish.

Pippa went to the stairs and ran her hand over the iron rail, the metal cold to the touch. Then she climbed the new staircase and let herself out onto the rooftop. Already the rails had been put up around the edge of the decking and a couple of lawn chairs sat in the center. Apparently someone had been enjoying some quality time up here.

Pippa settled onto one of the chairs and took in the view of the setting sun. And then she began to cry.

Chapter Eighteen

From somewhere deep inside a dream of skating on a ramp, a telephone shattered the silence. A second ring and Pippa reached blindly for the cell phone charging on her bedside table.

The clock on the phone read 4:25 a.m.

"Hello?" she managed through the fog of interrupted sleep.

"Pippa, it's Riley Burkett."

"What is it?" The thought occurred that she might still be dreaming. She waited to see what would happen next.

"You need to wake up," he said gently. "The warehouse is on fire."

She sat bolt upright. "Fire?"

"Yes," he said, and for the first time she noticed he sounded as if he was driving. "How do you know?"

"I got a call just now from Ryan Owen. The fire alarm was tripped. I told him I would call you and send you down there. So you need to go."

She threw off the blankets and somehow her feet found the floor. "Yes, all right. I'm getting dressed now. Are you there?"

"No. Susan and I are driving in from Houston right now."

Pippa tripped over the running shoes she'd left on the floor last night and then reached to snatch them up with her free hand. "And you're certain the warehouse is burning?"

"There could be a mistake," he admitted. "As you know, several of the properties down there look alike, though most of them are empty."

"Let's pray that if there is a fire it's one of the empty ones," she said. "And please drive safely."

After she hung up, Pippa threw on the first things she found: a pair of black running shorts, a sports bra and a long-sleeved black T-shirt emblazoned with the logo of the Houston Rockets basketball team.

Grabbing her bag, Pippa threw in her cell phone and palmed her keys, then stepped out into the early morning darkness. Though the warehouse was less than ten minutes away, she made it in just over five. As she turned the corner, the bright orange glow told her there was indeed a fire on the street. When she saw where the two Vine Beach Volunteer Fire Department trucks had parked, she knew the fire was at the headquarters of R10:14.

"Pippa?"

She turned toward the sound of the male voice, her sight blinded by the flash of red, blue and white emergency lights on the trucks and police cars.

"Pippa, over here."

Ryan Owen bounded toward her in full gear. "Riley says you're the key holder."

"I lease the building," she shouted over the sound of the truck engines.

He pushed back the visor on his gear to reveal his face. "Can you verify there's no one inside?"

"There shouldn't be," she said. "I was the last one out and I locked the door. The place was empty then."

"What time was that?"

"Still daylight," she said. "Maybe seven."

"It was 6:45."

Pippa turned to see Logan standing beside her. "She left here at 6:45."

"How do you know that?" Pippa demanded. "You left well before I did."

"Because I came back. And I waited." He turned to Ryan. "She and a kid named Rico Galvan left at 6:45 in his car. There were no other cars in the parking lot."

Ryan's attention went from Logan to Pippa and then back to Logan. "I'm going to need you to stick around," he told them both. "We'll need statements. And a list of anyone who was in or near the building today."

Someone called Ryan's name. "You two clear on what needs to be done?" When they both nodded, he raced back toward the inferno.

A policeman walked over to them. "Logan," he said, "you need to get her to a safe place until someone comes to take your statements."

"Come on." With his hand on her elbow, Logan guided Pippa away from the chaos and into his Jeep. The top was up, as were the windows, so sounds were muffled inside.

But colors weren't, and neither was the acrid scent of smoke.

"Any idea how this happened?" he finally asked.

"None."

Logan turned to face her. "Could it be one of those movie folks?"

"Movie folks?" She shook her head. "You mean the team filming the music video. No, of course not."

"They had plenty of electrical equipment. Generators and all kinds of electronics. You don't think maybe some of that set off a spark? Maybe fried the wires?"

"Impossible." She watched a flame shoot halfway to the moon, or so it seemed. A plume of water quickly swatted it back down.

"How so?"

Pippa forced her attention away from the awful scene. "Because they packed up everything before they left. You said you were here. Didn't you notice them filling the vans and rolling up wires and cords?"

"Yes, I did see that."

"What you saw was that film crew saving everything they brought out here plus all the banners Rico made." Tears, her companions earlier in the night, returned. "When I think of what could have been inside the building if Bryan didn't have the policy of keeping all the equipment under his control and not locking it into the location of the shoot…"

Pippa shook her head, speaking now impossible. The fire swam into an orange-and-black mess before her eyes as she allowed her tears to fall freely.

"Here." Logan put something soft in her hands. His sweatshirt. "It's clean, I promise."

Pippa almost smiled. Instead she buried her face in the soft soap-clean scent and wept. When Logan gathered her into his embrace, she did not protest. Instead she allowed the comfort.

Tomorrow she would think about how things stood with Logan. Right now she could not think at all.

As the sun rose on the ghoulish scene, it quickly became apparent there was nothing left to salvage. The warehouse and the ministry it sheltered were a total loss.

A small crowd had gathered, its numbers growing as word spread. A Houston television station's news truck pulled up with Riley Burkett right behind it. Logan used his free hand to open the driver's window and greet his father.

"Wasn't a bad escort," he said to Logan as he nodded toward the truck. "So, tell me what happened."

"Don't know yet," Logan said. "Not any more than what you told me anyway. No one was inside when Pippa and Rico left, and Pippa said the place was empty of anything that might cause a fire."

Riley looked past Logan to Pippa. "How're you doing, kid?"

"Not too well," she said with an embarrassing sniff. "But at least no one was hurt."

Riley nodded. "The owner has insurance, though I have to be honest with you, Pippa. I doubt he's going to rebuild."

"Oh."

A nod. "He's been wanting to rid himself of this building for years." Soon as he said the words, Riley straightened and Pippa could no longer see his face.

"Dad?" Logan stepped out to converse with his father in low tones. A moment later, Riley set off toward the cluster of emergency responders standing beside the fire marshal's vehicle.

When Logan did not immediately join her, Pippa climbed out to stand beside him. Before she could ask Logan about his conversation with his father, Ryan motioned for her to join him. "Okay, Pippa, I'm going to need a statement."

She followed Ryan to his truck and then allowed him to help her inside. "I'll send a man over in a second to ask the questions," he said as he closed the door and walked away.

From her vantage point, Pippa could see most of the film crew and all four band members gathered around

Bryan's Hummer. True to his nature, Chaz was filming the whole thing.

The rest of the morning went by in a blur of conversations, first with the fire inspector's assistant and then with a police officer. Finally a reporter from Channel 2 News stuck a microphone in Pippa's face and began grilling her.

When Bryan caught her distressed look, he bolted into action by hauling all four members of Romans Ten in front of the cameras to do an interview for the evening news about how the up-and-coming Christian band almost lost everything to a tragic fire. Then he pulled in Rico.

"Ask this guy about the ministry they run here. It's a fine organization, and this young man? He's not only second-in-command here, but he's also a talented artist. Did I mention he wants to become a preacher?" Bryan nodded to the reporter. "Go ahead and ask him about it."

Pippa marveled at the manager's ability to turn the situation around. As the reporter gave the signal to sign off, Bryan jumped back into the frame. "Wait just a minute, there's something else you need to tell your viewers."

The reporter pointed the microphone in his direction.

"I've just hung up with my banker. This ministry needs donations, folks, and here's what I'm going to do. We're setting up a fund in the name of R10:14 Ministries to help these kids rebuild. Call the station, viewers, and they'll have the information." At the reporter's worried look, Bryan gave her a comforting smile. "I've already emailed the information to your producer."

The crowd parted as a police officer made room. Behind him was Granny, perfectly coiffed and ready for her on-camera interview.

"Plans are already under way for a fund-raiser," Granny was saying. "My granddaughter is much better at planning these events than I am, but I can tell you that it will be held in the former Branson Building, soon to be the new home of Gallagher and Company. Our first order of business once the gallery opens is to have all of you in to bid on some wonderful art. I was just speaking with Mr. Rico Galvan, the young man you just interviewed. He is being quite generous in donating several of his art pieces to the auction."

The reporter kept the cameras rolling while Granny did a full quarter-hour interview and then promised to come into the studio in a few weeks to do a follow-up. And of course, during the whole thing, Chaz kept his camera rolling, as well.

At some point the kids began to arrive. Pippa's heart went out to the teens who wandered up or, in most instances skated up, their eyes bleary from sleep as they huddled together and watched their gathering place burn to the ground. Rico got to them before she could, and by the time Pippa reached the knot of kids, the Crossley twins were leading the group in prayer.

How long Pippa stayed at the scene of the fire, she had no idea. But when Ryan finally cleared her to leave, she didn't tarry. Instead she went home and once again found her bed, pulling her sheets over her head. Only when she woke sometime later, the sun slanting across the floor to blind her when she sat up, did she realize she was still wearing her running shoes.

Granny would not expect her at work today, so she didn't bother to make the attempt. Instead Pippa ran off down the beach to the lighthouse and back, a favorite morning exercise since she'd returned to Vine Beach. After a shower and a change into her favorite khaki shorts and the pink sweater she'd intended to wear to Galveston, Pippa opened her computer to read the news reports of the fire.

Her phone rang several times, but when the number on the caller ID was unfamiliar, she did not answer. Finally her stomach complained, and Pippa realized it was after two in the afternoon and she hadn't eaten.

The walls of the cabin beginning to press in around her, Pippa grabbed a bottle of water and an apple and went for a drive. She avoided the street where the warehouse now lay in shambles, and she also bypassed the Branson Building where Logan would likely be hard at work. Instead she turned toward Galveston and took a bite of the apple. Today was not a day to be in Vine Beach. Not anymore.

Pippa spent most of the afternoon walking on the seawall and poking around in the jumble of antiques shops clustered in the Strand area. She even made a point of driving down Broadway again just to see the name of that wedding facility in the big mansion.

The sun was setting when she finally returned to Vine Beach. Still, she didn't want to go home. No, that wasn't true. Pippa wanted to go to her new home. Or the home that would soon be hers.

So Pippa drove slowly up Main Street, promising herself she would stop only if Logan's Jeep wasn't parked out front. With no sign of him or Granny about, she parked and went inside. This time she didn't tarry but went straight up to the roof, where she sat in the same lawn chair and looked out at the same sunset.

So much had happened since this time yesterday. So much had changed.

Yesterday her complaint had been that Logan didn't support her ministry. Today her complaint was that the ministry was no more, at least for now.

It was a powerful lesson in being thankful for what a person might think was the worst thing that could happen. Because no matter how bad things got, they could always get worse.

Pippa glanced over her shoulder in the direction of where the warehouse once stood. When she spied the blackened smudge, she didn't bother to stop the tears that shimmered in her eyes. Instead she let them fall.

Who cared if she cried up here? No one but she and God were in the rooftop garden, and she felt His presence keenly.

"Pippa? Is that you, honey?"

"Granny?" She sniffed hard and swiped at her eyes with the tail of her T-shirt. "Yes, I'm up here."

Her grandmother appeared at the rooftop entrance, silver hair gleaming almost orange in the dimming light. She wore pale green linen trousers and a matching shirt, a strand of pearls at her throat. As usual, she looked stunning.

"How did you find me?"

"Sweetheart," Granny said, "you're the only person in Vine Beach with that car. And it *was* parked out front." She reached to pat Pippa's knee and spied the damage. "What have you done?"

Pippa told her the story all the way from the beginning until the moment when Logan patched her up, carefully leaving out the part where they'd argued. "But that was all yesterday. Today it doesn't seem to matter much."

They sat in silence for a moment and then Granny reached to grasp Pippa's hand. "This is just lovely, isn't it? The view looking out over the gulf."

"It is," she admitted.

"Have you figured out yet that the reason for this project was to get you back home?" Granny asked.

Pippa smiled. "It worked."

"Yes, it did. Proof positive the Lord answers prayers when He is of a mind to." Granny returned the gesture and then sobered. "The Burkett boy, he loves you, you know."

"Logan? No, Granny," she said softly. "He used to."

Her grandmother continued to look out at the ocean, a golden glow washing over her features as the sun slid farther toward the horizon. "What happened?"

"Stubbornness," a familiar male voice said.

Pippa looked up to see Logan stepping out of the roof-top entrance. "On whose part?"

"Well," Granny said, "my guess is it would be both of you." She rose and checked her watch. "And though you may believe this to be a coincidence, I am due downstairs to meet the McAlesters for dinner in exactly five minutes. It will take me at least that long to get all the way down and pretty up my lipstick."

"Coincidence?" Pippa shook her head.

"We don't believe in those," Logan supplied as Granny walked toward him, then paused just long enough to give him a hug.

When the door closed behind Granny, Pippa figured Logan would join her by seating himself in the empty chair. Or he might leave. Instead he remained right where he was, his back to the sunset and his face shadowed in darkness.

"A little late to be working up here," she finally said.

"I just came to straighten you out on something you said yesterday."

"Oh?"

He nodded. "Those kisses?"

She decided to take the bait. "What about them?"

"I'm still not sorry." He walked toward her then, tentative, as if she might not welcome his presence.

Maybe it was exhaustion or the lingering shock of the fire. Maybe it was the way the sunset cast everything in a different light up here. Or it might be the way he looked at her as he moved across the deck to stand before her.

Slowly he extended his hand. Even slower, she accepted it and rose.

And then he kissed her again.

"Forgive me," Logan said against her ear as he held her close. "I was a pigheaded man with a whole bunch of stupid ideas about how to do things."

"And I backed down from a fight we needed to have."

"We're quite a pair, aren't we?" Logan said. "What're we going to do about us?"

"You sure there's still an us?"

"Completely certain."

Pippa looked up at the man whose smile erased all the unpleasantness of the past twenty-four hours. "In that case, you're going to kiss me again, that's what."

And so he did.

Chapter Nineteen

"I can't believe August fifth is already here." Pippa put the finishing touches on the arrangement of lilies at the guest book table and then stepped away to admire her handiwork.

Logan had outdone himself in supervising the renovation of the ground floor of the Branson Building. Tomorrow was the gallery's official opening, but tonight was the fund-raiser Granny had promised back in May.

Rico's banners covered the walls of the expansive showroom, complemented by other pieces donated by artists from as far away as New York, Los Angeles and London. And in the corner, a small makeshift movie screen had been set up to air Romans Ten's debut video from their chart-topping single "Out of the Fire."

Though that hadn't been the name of the song when the boys played it at R10:14, the group added a few lines to reflect a verse in the book of Jude that referred to "snatching some from the fire."

Soon the guests began arriving, keeping Pippa and Granny busy making introductions. Riley and Susan Burkett exclaimed over the transformation, while Mayor Murdoch boasted that this was the beginning of an urban improvement that would transform the city.

Chaz arrived early in the evening, the 8 mm camera in tow. "Might have another video moment tonight," he said. "You just never know."

Soon after, Bryan parked the Hummer out front and the band members and several of the crew appeared. A second vehicle provided transport for the remainder of the group.

As much as the excitement centered on the music sensations, as the new artist whose works were being exhibited, Rico was the true star of the night. He arrived late, his eyes shining, and Pippa was the first person he sought out.

"Look," he said as he handed her an envelope. "I've been accepted to seminary."

Pippa grinned. "Just one?" she asked.

"Well, this is the one I chose," he said, "but yes, there were a few more."

They shared a laugh and then Rico sobered, something that concerned Pippa. "What's wrong?"

A shrug. "Funding," he said. "A scholarship might not kick in until next year since I was accepted so late."

She gave him a hug. "I don't think God's finished with this situation yet. Let's just see what He does."

"You know," Rico said softly, "I need to tell you something. I thought maybe I was the reason the warehouse burned."

"You?" Pippa shook her head. "Why would you say that?"

"I was working with all that paint and I thought maybe the fumes…" He shook his head. "Anyway, I'm glad that wasn't the case."

"It wasn't the fault of the band or video crew, either," she said. "I know that was a concern, too."

Rico shrugged. "The building was old and apparently

so was the wiring. I guess it was a good coincidence that it happened when everyone was away from it."

"And everything," Pippa said as she nodded to the banners now being admired by the guests. "Or almost everything. I hated losing the ramps and other things, but I suppose they're all replaceable should we ever be able to reopen the ministry in someplace other than a borrowed venue." She gave Rico a no-nonsense look. "But you know what I say about coincidences."

"Yeah, sorry. We don't believe in them, do we?"

"Exactly. Now go greet your adoring fans. It looks like you've got a line of people waiting to meet the artist."

Rico moved on to speak to one of Granny's many friends, and Pippa set out to find Bryan Feldman. When she spied him speaking to the Crossley twins and their father, she joined them. After a moment, Pippa looked to Bryan. "Can I see you for just a minute?"

They made their excuses to the Crossleys and then Pippa led him over to a quiet corner and pulled out the business card he had given her the day before the video shoot. "Remember that favor?"

Bryan nodded. "What's it going to cost me?"

She whispered the amount in his ear, and his eyebrows rose. "Dare I ask what this is for and how I'm to deliver this amount of money?"

Pippa nodded to the corner where Rico's banners would soon be auctioned off. "I know this artist who just got accepted to seminary. Unfortunately his scholarship won't kick in until next year."

"Well, then, if you'll excuse me, I need to see an auctioneer about a banner." Bryan shook his head. "For that amount, I'd better be able to buy all of them."

"There you are." Logan came up behind Pippa and

wrapped his arm around her. "The place looks beauti-ful." He kissed her cheek. "And so do you."

"Thank you," Pippa whispered. "Only for you."

He smiled. "I have a little something to show you. One last construction detail."

"Ladies and gentlemen," Granny said, "if you'll gather here, I would like very much to get the bidding started."

Eric Wilson and his wife, Amy, moved past, and Amy paused to hug Pippa. "I'm so excited to see what God will do with the money we raise tonight. The kids are doing well gathering at the church, but I know they will be hap-pier once they get their own place again."

Pippa agreed and then accepted a hug from Eric be-fore releasing them to go and stand among those who were waiting to bid. She spied Leah Owen in the crowd and waved.

"I should tell you," Logan said, "your friend Leah and I are going to be seeing more of each other."

"What?" She turned to face Logan and saw Ryan standing next to him.

"It's fine," the fire chief said. "He has my complete permission. In fact, I'm the one who asked."

Pippa shook her head. "What are you talking about?"

Logan grinned. "I'm going to be in charge of the reno-vations at Berryhill. Actually," he corrected, "it's really more of a complete do-over, to use a technical term, since the fire took out much of the original place."

Ryan clapped his hand on Logan's shoulder. "If anyone can make that happen, it's your Logan. I keep telling him he needs to stop playing around and get that architectural degree." He looked over at the young foreman. "Just not until after you're finished with Berryhill, okay?"

Logan shook his head and then watched as Ryan went

to join his wife. "So," he said when he returned his attention to Pippa. "What do you think?"

"I think it's a great idea," she said. "And I promise I did not put him up to telling you that you should become an architect."

"I did wonder. So, about that thing I wanted to show you." He nodded to the stairs. "If we don't go now, we're going to get stuck in the speech-giving. And I know how you love to stick around for all the festivities. Time to make our escape again."

She looked up into smiling eyes. "Logan Burkett, you are something."

"That's what you love about me." He grabbed her hand. "Come on."

Pippa followed Logan up the stairs and into the loft she had finally moved the remainder of her things into this morning. "What is it?"

He gestured to the spiral staircase. "Up there," he said, "but you'll have to wear this." Logan pulled a length of black silk from his pocket. "Otherwise it will spoil the surprise," he said when she gave him an I-don't-think-so look.

His soft "Trust me" was her undoing, and she allowed him to put the mask in place, then ease her up the staircase and out into the summer night.

Shuffling along in three-inch heels wasn't easy, but Pippa managed it. Finally Logan stopped. "Okay, I'm going to turn you around." He helped her down onto what felt like some kind of park bench.

"Don't peek," he said, and a band began to play a soft jazzy number.

"Oh, that's nice, Logan," she said, "but I'm getting a little nervous about what you're up to. Can I take the blindfold off now?"

"Yes, Pippa, take off the blindfold."

What she saw when the silk fell away took Pippa's breath. The rooftop deck had been transformed into a beautiful nighttime wonderland. Candles flickered from every surface and strands of white lights crisscrossed overhead illuminating the completed patio.

She looked over to see that the band she had heard playing the soft romantic music was Romans Ten. Rather than their plaid-shirt grunge attire, all four were decked out in matching tuxedos.

"Very nice," she called, and the drummer winked.

Pippa looked up and saw that not only had Logan incorporated an arbor into his design; he had somehow entwined it with pink climbing roses and more sparkling white lights.

"It's beautiful," she whispered. "Just perfect."

"No, Pippa, you are," he said. "Beautiful, and perfect… for me."

He knelt before her and presented her with a Tiffany blue box.

"Logan?"

"Open it," he said, and when she did, he lifted an exquisite diamond ring out and placed it on her finger. "Be my wife, Pippa?" he asked.

"Yes," she said with a smile. Then she spied a piece of folded paper at the bottom of the box. "But what's this?"

"Just a little something for you," he said.

She unfolded the paper and found a drawing. "It's a skate park."

"And ministry headquarters," he said. "Of course, the design is just a suggestion. I thought maybe you and I could finalize the plans together."

Pippa shook her head. "But where? I mean we don't have a place to put this."

"We do, sweetheart. This afternoon I had the machine shop razed. There's an empty lot just waiting to be built on." He paused to meet her gaze. "And in the meantime I thought maybe the kids would like to put a ramp out there. Maybe do some skating?"

"But what if I get hurt? I can't promise I won't skate occasionally."

Logan shrugged. "Can't be worrying about what *might* happen when I'm busy thanking the Lord for what *is* happening, right?"

"Right." Gathering him into an embrace, Pippa did her best not to cry. "You've made me so happy, Logan. Truly."

He shook his head. "I'm glad to hear it, but I'm not done yet." He walked over to the edge of the building and whistled.

"What are you doing?"

Logan motioned for her to remain in place. "Just hang on, sweetheart. I think you're really going to like this last construction detail."

Pippa laughed. "All right."

A loud diesel engine sprang to life down on the street and then a strange beeping noise began. At the same time, guests from the party downstairs began filing through the door to join them on the roof. Still the beeping continued.

Then, slowly, something appeared above the rail. Something yellow and…it looked like a crane. "Logan?"

He shook his head. "Patience."

A wire had been suspended from the end of the crane, and at the end of the wire she spied something red. Slowly the crane continued to lift the object until finally Pippa realized what it was.

"The British phone box!" she exclaimed. "The one from the salvage yard!"

"That's right," he said as the crane operator moved the phone box into place atop a large black X that had been painted onto the decking.

"There you are, Pippa," Logan said. Of course Chaz captured it all on video. And so did Channel 2 News.

* * * * *

Dear Reader,

Do you love the beach as much as I do? I'm so glad! If I had my way, there would be no winter, only lovely late spring weather and sandy beaches to lounge on. Oh, but that would be wonderful, wouldn't it?

I'm thrilled to get one more chance to write about my favorite fictional Texas beach town, Vine Beach. Since I began this series, I can close my eyes and walk the streets of Vine Beach in my mind.

When I set out to write Logan and Pippa's story, I knew I wanted to write about perceptions, about how as humans we are quick to form opinions that are not always accurate. God tells us we are new creatures in Him and that His mercies are new every morning. I don't know about you, but I hold tightly to those promises, and so do the characters in this novel.

If anything you have read in this novel has touched you regarding these kids, please prayerfully consider supporting ministries such as Christian Skaters (www.christianskaters.com) or Skate Bible (www.skatebible.com) that reach the skating community for Christ. And lest you see someone and think that you know them, remember what the Lord said to Samuel in 1 Samuel 16:7: *"Do not consider his appearance...The Lord does not look at the things people look at. People look at the outward appearance, but the Lord looks at the heart."*

Kathleen Y'Barbo

Questions for Discussion

1. Logan has returned to Vine Beach to sell a piece of property he inherited after his wife died and then he will leave town for good. What he doesn't take into account is the fact that God has other plans for him. Have you ever made plans only to find out the Lord intended something else? What did you do?

2. Pippa feels a special need to reach out to kids who do not fit in because she recalls what that felt like when she was a teenager. Do you have life experiences that the Lord is using? If so, how? If not, can you call upon anything in your past that you might use to help others?

3. The renovation of the Branson Building moves along at approximately the same pace as the relationship between Pippa and Logan. Some moments are rocky, while others are quite smooth and pleasant. Your relationship with God can be that way, too. Where are you in your walk with God? Could your relationship with Him use some renovation? If so, in what areas?

4. Pippa grew up as the child of missionaries serving in Asia and then came back to live with her grandmother as a high school student. This was a huge change for her, one that had a lasting effect. Has God called on you to make a big change? If so, what was it and how did it affect you?

5. Logan Burkett's father resorted to drastic measures to try and save him when he was an errant teenager. At the time, Logan did not feel this was the act of

a father who cared for him. Have you felt this way about your heavenly Father? If so, why and what did you do about it?

6. Pippa and Logan have hobbies that are similar, and yet Logan is too stubborn to admit it. Do you battle with a stubborn streak? What have you done to try to overcome the habit?

7. Early in the book, Pippa and Logan visit a salvage shop where people can reclaim and reuse discarded items. How does this idea of reclaiming apply to our hearts? Are you allowing the Lord to reclaim your heart and use it for His purposes? If not, what is stopping you?

8. Pippa allows Rico to paint the warehouse and to create a logo for R10:14 that looks like street art. She feels this will reach kids who might not otherwise come to the skate park. What do you think of ministries' attempts to use popular culture to spread the Gospel? Can you give an example?

9. Logan is hard on teens because he feels someone needs to guide them before all is lost. Does his tough love approach make sense to you or are you more attuned to reaching people Pippa's way? While neither option is wrong, why is your option right for you? Can you give an example of a time you used this method? How did it turn out?

10. When the skate park is destroyed, Logan sets his feelings aside and comes to help. Could you have done what he did? Have you ever had to make a choice like his? If so, what did you do and why?

11. Logan blames himself for his wife's death and carries a heavy amount of guilt because of this. Are you burdened with guilt? What can you do today to relieve that feeling and make a fresh start with the Lord?

12. Pippa and Logan overcome seemingly insurmountable odds to fall in love and commit to a relationship that will culminate in marriage. What is it you need to overcome today? How will you manage it? What is God's part in this process and what is your part?

COMING NEXT MONTH FROM
Love Inspired®

Available July 15, 2014

HIS MONTANA SWEETHEART
Big Sky Centennial • by Ruth Logan
Olivia Franklin never imagined coming home would mean running into
first love Jack McGuire. Can working together on the town's centennial
celebration give these former sweethearts a second chance at forever?

THE AMISH NANNY
Brides of Amish Country • by Patricia Davids
Schoolteacher Clara Barkman has no plans to wed. But when she's
hired by handsome Ethan Gingerich to care for his orphaned niece and
nephews, she can't resist the tug on her heartstrings!

A HEART TO HEAL
Gordon Falls • by Allie Pleiter
Counselor Heather Browning isn't used to living on the edge, but when
she teams up with adventure-seeking Max Jones to help a struggling teen,
will she risk putting her heart on the line?

BLUE RIDGE REUNION
Barrett's Mill • by Mia Ross
Old rivals Chelsea Barnes and Paul Barrett clashed over everything. But as
they work together to repair the landmark mill in their hometown, soon the
only thing they're fighting for is a future together.

THE WIDOWER'S SECOND CHANCE
Goose Harbor • by Jessica Keller
Paige Windom moves to picturesque Goose Harbor to find an escape—not
romance. But while working with fellow teacher Caleb Beck to help inner-
city teens, she'll find the handsome widower hard to resist.

LONE STAR HERO
by Jolene Navarro
Separated by their families decades before, former sweethearts
Jake Torres and Vickie Lawson reunite to help her troubled son and
discover that a perfect love is worth waiting for.

**LOOK FOR THESE AND OTHER LOVE INSPIRED BOOKS WHEREVER
BOOKS ARE SOLD, INCLUDING MOST BOOKSTORES, SUPERMARKETS,
DISCOUNT STORES AND DRUGSTORES.**

LICNM0714

REQUEST YOUR FREE BOOKS!

2 FREE INSPIRATIONAL NOVELS
PLUS 2 FREE MYSTERY GIFTS

Love Inspired

YES! Please send me 2 FREE Love Inspired® novels and my 2 FREE mystery gifts (gifts are worth about $10). After receiving them, if I don't wish to receive any more books, I can return the shipping statement marked "cancel." If I don't cancel, I will receive 6 brand-new novels every month and be billed just $4.74 per book in the U.S. or $5.24 per book in Canada. That's a saving of at least 21% off the cover price. It's quite a bargain! Shipping and handling is just 50¢ per book in the U.S. and 75¢ per book in Canada.* I understand that accepting the 2 free books and gifts places me under no obligation to buy anything. I can always return a shipment and cancel at any time. Even if I never buy another book, the two free books and gifts are mine to keep forever.

105/305 IDN F47Y

Name _____ (PLEASE PRINT) _____

Address _____ Apt. # _____

City _____ State/Prov. _____ Zip/Postal Code _____

Signature (if under 18, a parent or guardian must sign)

Mail to the Harlequin® Reader Service:
IN U.S.A.: P.O. Box 1867, Buffalo, NY 14240-1867
IN CANADA: P.O. Box 609, Fort Erie, Ontario L2A 5X3

**Are you a subscriber to Love Inspired books
and want to receive the larger-print edition?
Call 1-800-873-8635 or visit www.ReaderService.com.**

* Terms and prices subject to change without notice. Prices do not include applicable taxes. Sales tax applicable in N.Y. Canadian residents will be charged applicable taxes. Offer not valid in Quebec. This offer is limited to one order per household. Not valid for current subscribers to Love Inspired books. All orders subject to credit approval. Credit or debit balances in a customer's account(s) may be offset by any other outstanding balance owed by or to the customer. Please allow 4 to 6 weeks for delivery. Offer available while quantities last.

Your Privacy—The Harlequin® Reader Service is committed to protecting your privacy. Our Privacy Policy is available online at www.ReaderService.com or upon request from the Harlequin Reader Service.

We make a portion of our mailing list available to reputable third parties that offer products we believe may interest you. If you prefer that we not exchange your name with third parties, or if you wish to clarify or modify your communication preferences, please visit us at www.ReaderService.com/consumerschoice or write to us at Harlequin Reader Service Preference Service, P.O. Box 9062, Buffalo, NY 14269. Include your complete name and address.

LI13R

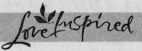
Don't miss a single book in the
BIG SKY CENTENNIAL *miniseries!*
Will rancher Jack McGuire and former love
Olivia Franklin find happily ever after in
HIS MONTANA SWEETHEART by Ruth Logan Herne?
Here's a sneak peek:

"We used to count the stars at night, Jack. Remember that?"

Oh, he remembered, all right. They'd look skyward and watch each star appear, summer, winter, spring and fall, each season offering its own array, a blend of favorites. Until they'd become distracted by other things. Sweet things.

A sigh welled from somewhere deep within him, a quiet blooming of what could have been. "I remember."

They stared upward, side by side, watching the sunset fade to streaks of lilac and gray. Town lights began to appear north of the bridge, winking on earlier now that it was August. "How long are you here?"

Olivia faltered. "I'm not sure."

He turned to face her, puzzled.

"I'm between lives right now."

He raised an eyebrow, waiting for her to continue. She did, after drawn-out seconds, but didn't look at him. She kept her gaze up and out, watching the tree shadows darken and dim.

"I was married."

He'd heard she'd gotten married several years ago, but the "was" surprised him. He dropped his gaze to her left hand. No ring. No tan line that said a ring had been there

LIEXP0714

this summer. A flicker that might be hope stirred in his chest, but entertaining those notions would get him nothing but trouble, so he blamed the strange feeling on the half-finished sandwich he'd wolfed down on the drive in.

You've eaten fast plenty of times before this and been fine. Just fine.

The reminder made him take a half step forward, just close enough to inhale the scent of sweet vanilla on her hair, her skin.

He shouldn't. He knew that. He knew it even as his hand reached for her hand, the left one bearing no man's ring, and that touch, the press of his fingers on hers, made the tiny flicker inside brighten just a little.

The surroundings, the trees, the thin-lit night and the sound of rushing water made him feel as if anything was possible, and he hadn't felt that way in a very long time. But here, with her?

He did. And it felt good.

Find out what else is going on in Jasper Gulch in HIS MONTANA SWEETHEART by Ruth Logan Herne, available August 2014 from Love Inspired®.

Love Inspired

A reclusive Amish logger, Ethan Gingerich is more comfortable around his draft horses than the orphaned niece and nephews he's taken in. Yet he's determined to provide the children with a good, loving home. The little ones, including a defiant eight-year-old, need a proper nanny. But when Ethan hires shy Amishwoman Clara Barkman, he never expects her temporary position to have such a lasting hold on all of them. Now this man of few words must convince Clara she's found her forever home and family.

BRIDES OF
Amish Country

Finding true love in the land of the Plain People.

The Amish Nanny

by

Patricia Davids

*Available August 2014 wherever
Love Inspired books and ebooks are sold.*

LI87902